On A Good Day

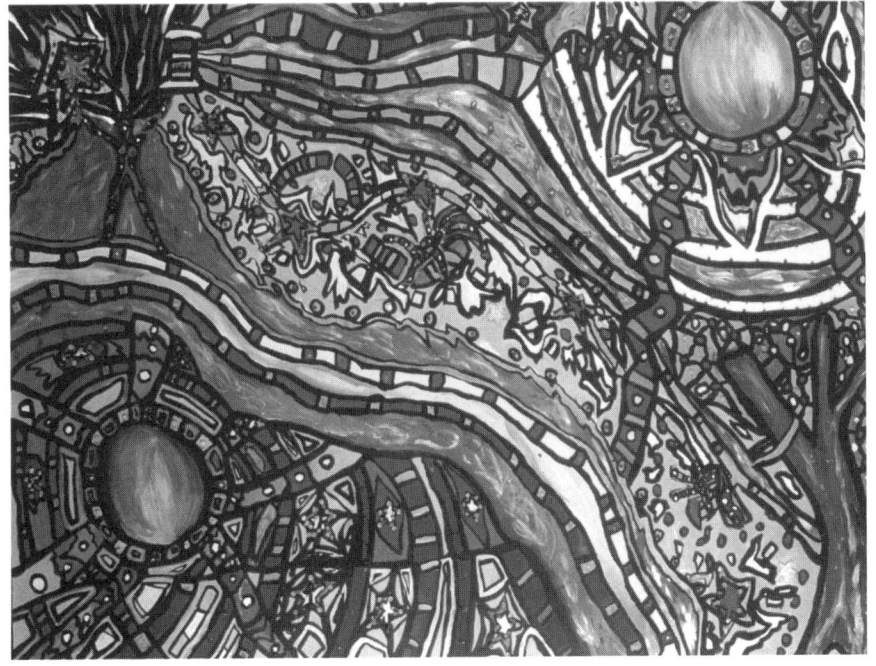

Gay Rubin

Plain View Press
P. O. 33311
Austin, TX 78764
Phone/Fax: 512-441-2452

e-mail: sbpvp@eden.com
Website: http://www.eden.com/~sbpvp
1-800-878-3605

ISBN: 0-911051-96-1
Library of Congress Number: 97-069879

Second edition copyright, Gay Rubin, 1998. All rights reserved.
First edition copyright 1992 by Gay Rubin. No part of this book may be mimeographed or reproduced, other than for reviews, without the expressed permission of the author or Plain View Press.

Acknowledgments

Some of these stories originally appeared, some in different forms, in the following: "Looking for Paul Newman," *The Metro Times First Annual Summer Fiction Issue,* 1988. "My Mother's Sapphires," *The Bridge,* fall 1990. "If It's a Good Day, One Thing," *The Bridge,* spring/summer 1991.

Cover Art

The cover painting is by award-winning artist Rebecca Rubin. She attends Cranbrook/Kingswood High School and will soon travel to Costa Rica to do community service work in the rain forest.

Section Photo Identification

Black and white photos of art by Rebecca Rubin: *Journey,* ink (page 8); *Doll,* jewelry (page 17); *Good Day,* acrylic (page 22); *Untitled,* ink (page 34); *Aunt Molly,* acrylic and ink (page 40); *Untitled,* fabric and acrylic (page 46); *Detroit,* ink (page 56).

Thanks

The author wishes to thank The Ragdale Foundation for time and space to work. She also wishes to thank, for their advice and encouragement, C. Michael Curtis, Nicholas Delbanco, Richard Elman, Gordon Lish, and the group of Detroit poets she meets with once a month. Thanks also to Margo LaGattuta and Plain View Press.

This is a second edition. The first edition was published in 1992, in Detroit, Michigan, by The Ridgeway Press.

On a Good Day

a collection of short fiction by Gay Rubin

For Fred, Jessica, and Rebecca

Contents

Looking for Paul Newman   7

My Mother's Sapphires   15

If It's a Good Day, One Thing   21

An Ordinary Ride Up an Old Trail   33

His Mother's Piano   39

Last Chance Louie   45

Howie the Bum   55

Looking for Paul Newman

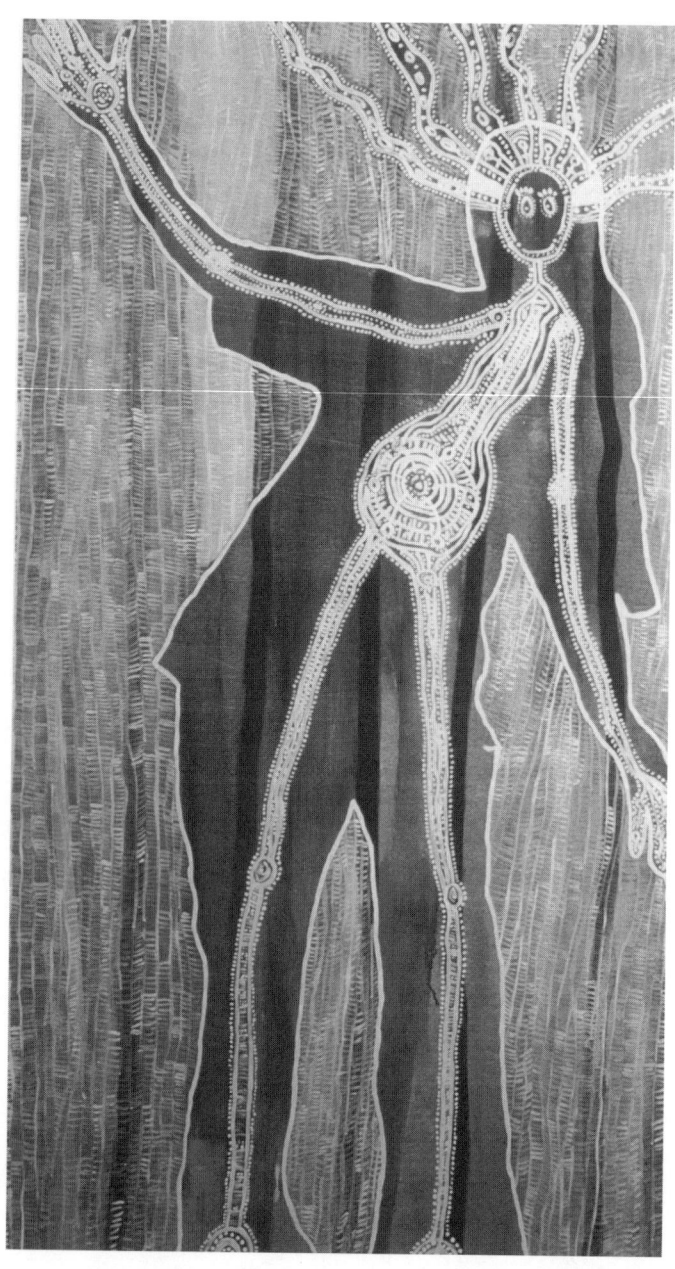

The first person here in Detroit who told me she had seen Paul Newman in person told me he was very short. My friend is not short. She is almost the same height as her first husband, who once played basketball for the Pistons. "Believe me," she said. "One thing I know, height doesn't mean a thing when you're lying down."

Did she lie down with him, I wanted to ask her, but that was the moment our daughters danced onto the stage dressed as birds and tapped the toes of their black, patent-leather shoes and sang "Glo Little Glo Worm, Glimmer, Glimmer."

"Did you?" I asked.

"I'll tell you about it later," she whispered. But after our daughters flapped their wings goodbye to the audience, they tiptoed off the stage, down the aisle, and found our laps in the dark.

I asked, "What did he eat?"

"The house specialty," she whispered. She waited for a pause between acts to tell me what it was. "A divine chicken sauté with walnuts in a sherry sauce," she said. "I had it too. And for dessert he had the chocolate torte, and he drank real coffee, not decaffinated. Believe me, I was close to him. I saw everything. I saw the ring he wore on his pinky. A star sapphire."

"But, what did he say?" I asked.

"Call me." she said. "We'll have lunch. Maybe next week."

I didn't have to wait a week to talk about Paul Newman. The next morning my housekeeper, Althea, came in to do the laundry and showed me pictures she took of him at the Grand Prix. There were close-up, full-body shots of Paul Newman in a racing suit. There were close-up face shots of his white teeth and his blue eyes.

"Not bad," she said. "I mean the focus, don't you think?"

"The lighting, too," I said. "Back lit, hair glowing. You must have used a zoom lense."

"Uh, uh. I moved in close. I wasn't three feet away from him."

"But how?" I asked. "How did you get that close?"

"I just walked up to him," she said. "He was standing there, and I said, can I take your picture, and he said sure."

"How does he look?" I asked.

"Like that. He looks just like his picture."

"But is he tall?"

"Sort of."

Althea doesn't know anything about tall. She stands on a chair to reach the low shelf in the kitchen. Almost everything looks high-up to her.

"What about his eyes?" I asked.

"Just like in the picture. That lighting really is good, isn't it?"

Althea's pictures of Paul Newman were much better than the ones on the cover of *National Enquirer* the next week. Right after I didn't buy the *National Enquirer* at the grocery store, I went to my dentist's office, and that is where I saw Paul Newman get into an elevator. It was his racing jacket and his hair that I saw. So I ran to the elevator. My heels made noises like the beats of a small drum, and my bronze necklace fell forward and back against my chest as I ran, so the hammered disks hit each other and sounded like miniature tamborines. All the people in the elevator were looking at me. Their eyes were wide and startled when I reached them. The door began to close. "Hold that elevator," I shouted. "Emergency." A man who wasn't Paul Newman, a man with brown eyes and a grey suit, grabbed the door and held it open. My necklace made music, as I squeezed myself and my big, bulky purse into the over-packed elevator. All the people pushed to the back and squeezed themselves tighter together. Some of them sighed and rolled their eyes to the ceiling, and some of them sighed and shrugged. I thought this meant that they felt inconvenienced but were understanding.

"What floor?" the man who wasn't Paul Newman asked.

"How many floors are there?" I asked.

The looks on everybody's faces changed. I won't tell you what they said. I didn't care what they said. I was looking for Paul Newman. I searched in the clutch of squashed-together people for the white hair and the red and silver racing jacket. I found the hair and the jacket, but they were on a boy. A youngster. Maybe 15 years old. There was nothing to do but ride up to the 25th floor and back down again.

After I saw my dentist, I went back to the grocery store, and I bought the *National Enquirer*. The story in the *National Enquirer* said that Paul Newman drank 92 bottles of beer at a horse show in Santa Barbara.

I called my horsey, second-cousin Sandra, who lives in California. She said his daughter was in the show; that is why Paul was there. He was watching his daughter, and he wasn't drinking beer, it was spring water. She said it wasn't even 92 bottles of spring water, but she could see why they changed it for the article. A bottle of spring water. What kind of story was that?

The next time I was at the grocery store, I bought spring water. While I was loading my cart with bottles of it, I saw my tall friend. She shouted, "I've been calling you and calling you. Where have you been?" So I pushed my cart closer to hers. "We've got to get together for lunch," she said. "I want to tell you about my dream." She moved closer to me. Almost whispered, "In my dream God spoke to me."

"What did He say?"

"Call me," she said. "We'll have lunch. I'll tell you everything."

"Just tell me one thing. Was He tall?"

"No," she said. "He looked like Paul Newman, but without hair."

When I drank the spring water, I noticed an increase in energy. I noticed less irritability. I started dancing in the shower. I didn't think about Paul Newman again until I was waiting in line at the travel agent's. At the travel agent's, I always think about the kind of things I think about at a funeral. Buying airline tickets and going to a funeral are the same thing to me. So what I thought about were the millions of people who would see Paul Newman. He would visit dreams all over the world, and his voice would be the voice of God, and I would never hear it.

I bought more spring water. I bought several brands. From France. From Germany. From Poland Springs, Maine. From Plymouth, Michigan.

I drank the spring water until there was nothing left to do but get on the plane. Then my daughter asked me why we had to meet Uncle Joe's new wife. I said, maybe we didn't. Maybe we could forget the whole thing. But it was too late. They were showing the movie that tells you what to do with your floatable seat cushion when the plane falls into an ocean. I asked the stewardess if she had any spring water. She said she had Seven-Up or club soda. I said I'd take vodka, and I drank that until we landed.

When we got off the plane, my feet were heavy, and I walked slowly. Mindy, the bird, skipped and shouted, "There they are, there they are," and there they were, a pretty woman in a red dress and my brother, Joe. Joe's new wife made a fuss over Mindy. She sat next to her in the backseat and told airplane stories all the way to the Westport Hotel. She flies all the time. She never gets tired. Not like me. I was going to rest as soon as we carried in our bags, but then Joe said he had errands to run. He said he had to pick up his shirts at the shirt laundry, and do some other things, did I want to go with him? I said no, but he said, "Sometimes I run into Paul Newman. He lives here in town, you know. He takes his shirts to the same place I do."

So of course I went. And of course I saw Paul Newman. "There he is. Look. Turning left at that light. Look at him," I shouted.

But Joe said, "Uh uh, he doesn't drive a Jag."
"What's he drive?"
"I don't know. It's small and dark."
"That Jag is small and dark."
"That's not him."

"Oh, come on, follow that car."

"It's a waste," he said, but he turned anyway, and we followed the car until it stopped in front of a white house with green shutters, and a man who was not Paul Newman got out.

Then we backtracked to the shirt laundry, and just as we parked our car, a man who looked like Paul Newman, exactly like Paul Newman, left the shirt laundry, carrying his shirts on a hanger, and got into a small dark car.

"That was him," Joe said. "We just missed him."

"My whole life is like this," I said.

Joe looked at me the way he used to when he was winning at Monopoly. "All right," he said. "We'll eat dinner at Provencino's on Sunday night. Paul Newman always eats dinner there on Sunday nights, and I'll reserve the table next to the one he reserves, and you'll see him." And Joe did what he said, and we went, all the out-of-towners, the cousins, the aunts and uncles, the nieces and nephews, to Provencino's, and Paul Newman didn't, and it didn't matter, because when I told my tall friend about it, I told her he did. I told her I couldn't help staring. I knew it was wrong, but I couldn't stop, and then he stared back. In fact our eyes locked, while we were eating spaghetti. I told her it was embarrassing, but then he took a gold pen from his breast pocket and wrote something on his napkin. Then he rolled the napkin into a ball, spit on it, and shot it under the table so it landed at my feet. I told her I went to the ladies room to read it in private.

"What did it say, what did it say?" she wanted to know. I told her it was a phone number. I said that under the phone number he had written, *Call me. Any Wednesday morning.* I told her he signed his name. She wanted to know what he said when I called him. So I told her he asked me to meet him in Manhattan at a little restaurant in the village. I did, and we had a drink. I told her I had Perrier, and he had a Heineken's Light. I told her he wore a cowboy hat, dark glasses and blue jeans, so nobody would recognize him, but people did anyway. One person came up to him and asked for his autograph, while we were drinking. "And then, and then?" she wanted to know. So I told her we went to an apartment, a large high-ceilinged place with wood floors, Indian rugs, lots of bookcases and plants and leather couches. We had another drink, and then we made love.

"You're making this up," she said.

"You're right. I didn't go to bed with him," I said. "I didn't even call him back."

"Why not?" she slapped her hand on the table, leaned forward.

I said, "Are you kidding? I don't want to end up in that position with Paul Newman. But I do like having his phone number, just in case."

My Mother's Sapphires

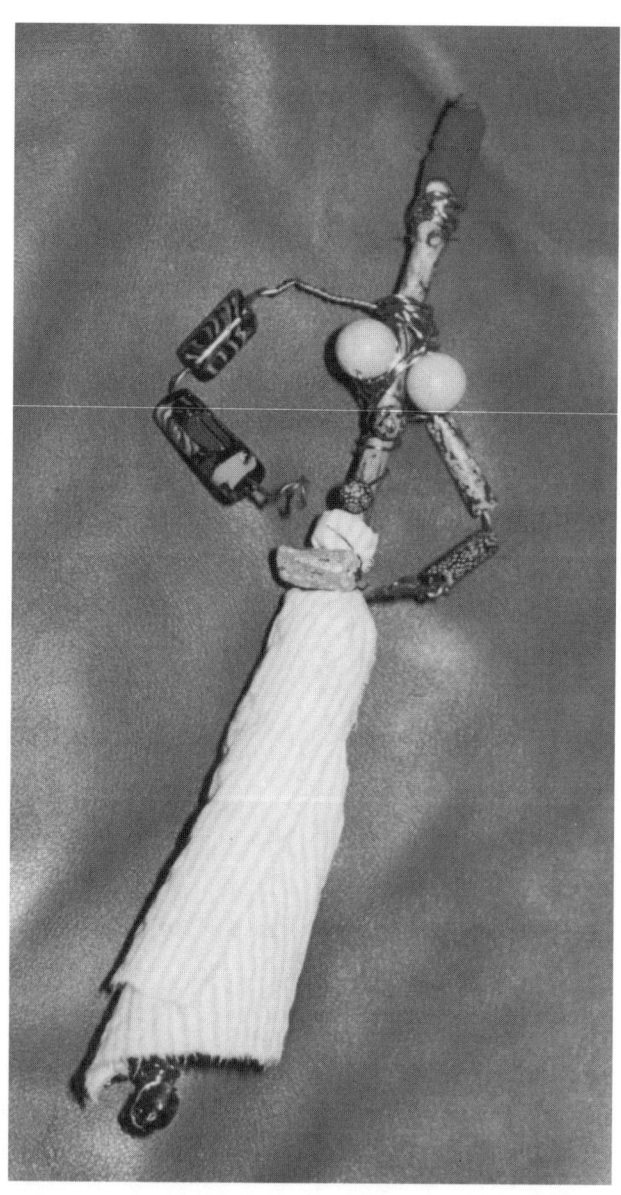

I thought my mother was a witch and had cast a spell on my father. The spell made him disappear, all except for his eyes. His eyes were in a box on her dressing table. She said they were earrings. Star sapphires she called them, and she stuck them through the holes pierced in her ears when she got dressed up. She got dressed up when she went out with men who were not my father. And when she did, she always wore something black, black and thin. I mean thin to her body, so she looked to me like a long, black tube. It wasn't only the darkness and the thinness of her that made her look like a witch. It was the sapphires. When I saw her with the sapphires, I thought of what she did to my father, and it made me feel like when I was high up on a ladder, and I looked down, and I felt like I was going to fall off. But I wanted to see her with the sapphires anyway. I wanted to see her with them so badly that if a friend asked me over to play, I said no. I said no, even if the friend asked me to sleep over. I said no, even if the friend had tickets to the Shrine circus, if I knew my mother was going to get dressed up and go out with a man who wasn't my father. I would stay home and beg, "Oh please, I promise to be quiet, promise, promise," and I would sit on the floor and not say anything, while she twirled on the stool at her vanity. She didn't like it when I twirled, but she always did, and when she did she pulled her feet up off the floor, and pointed her toes, and kept her back very straight like a ballet dancer's. Then she would stop twirling, and she would slowly and carefully scrunch up her black pantyhose, so they looked like one black thing and not two. Then she would point the toes of one foot and put the pointed foot into the scrunched up toe of one of the sides of her pantyhose, and then she would slowly pull the black shadow up over her leg, so it was a black shadow leg, and then she did the same thing with her other leg, so she'd have two black shadow legs. And then she would put her feet into her black shoes with the tall, skinny heels and the pointed toes, and then she would put on her shiny, black slip with the very tiny roses on the straps. And when she started to look like a long, black tube, she would pull the rubber bands out of her braid, and her hair would squiggle out as if it was really a thousand caterpillars, instead of hair, and when she moved her head, they moved too. They crawled out of the tightness they were in together in her braid and went all over her shoulders. But I didn't say anything. If I had even made a squeak or a grunt in the back of my throat, I knew she would have sent me away, and I wouldn't have been able to watch her paint on her witch's face. I wouldn't have seen her take the big brush with the fat, bushy tail out of the tall cup and dip it in the pot full of golden brown powder. I wouldn't have seen her take that brush full of brown powder and spread it over her cheeks, and her forehead, and her chin, and then I wouldn't have seen her coat the short, tiny brush with silvery powder and then paint the silvery powder onto her eyelids. And then I'd never see her take a red pencil and outline her lips with red. I'd never see her pout like a pretty-lady on television, while she outlined her lips, and then finally do what she always did for ordinary days, when she wasn't dressed up and going out with a man who wasn't my father. What she always did for ordinary days was she took an ordinary tube of lipstick, and she put the lipstick on her lips the way all the other mothers did, the mothers who weren't witches. So I stayed quieter and quieter, so I could be there for the finish, when she looked in the mirror and smiled and said "What do you think?" and I would say, "Good." But I meant, good for a witch's face.

That is when she would reach over and pull the box with the sapphires in it toward her. And that is when I would close my eyes and hold my breath, just for a second, because I really didn't want to miss seeing her do what she did next. What she did next was to take first one sapphire out of the box and put it in her ear, and then the other sapphire out of the box and put it in her other ear. Every time I saw her do that I would be dizzy the way I was dizzy at the carnival after spinning on the Tilt-a-Whirl, and I would close my eyes and lean against the wall. But then I would open my eyes and look at the stars in my mother's ears, and I would see them giving off light in the mirror. And the tiny diamonds that were all around the stars would give off light too, and I thought the light they gave off looked like laughter, and I thought that it was my father's eyes laughing. And then my mother would look at her watch and say, "Oh, dear, it's almost time," and then she would get all fluttery and wave her hands in the air and brush at her lap as if there were crumbs. Then she would stand up and she would hold her dress still at the hips, and she would wiggle so that her body moved and the dress didn't, and then she would stand still and smooth her dress on the sides and the front, and then she would look in the mirror, and she would sigh, and the sigh would have a trill in it like a song, and I thought she was singing because she could hear my father laughing in her ears. I thought if he laughed in her ears enough times, she would know how much he loved her, and she would bring him back.

If It's a Good Day, One Thing

Lately, my father complains about losing things. He calls me on the phone to tell me what he's lost. Money in the stock market. Keys to his car. Keys to the office he doesn't go to anymore. Important papers. Documents. Last week, he lost an enemy. The guy, Bernie Wolfgang, said to him, let's have lunch. Let's bury the hatchet. Why not? Dad said no, but even when he didn't go, he still counted the offer as a loss. It depressed him, he said, to see the old alligator lose his teeth. I said maybe Bernie hasn't lost his teeth, maybe he's just gotten sense, but Dad was deaf to it. I don't know what to do. He doesn't even want to lose weight. Two pounds, and he's on the phone with me. Adding up his losses. I joke about it. I say, the only person in America who doesn't want to lose weight. He says "What?" I say, "THE ONLY PERSON IN AMERICA WHO DOESN'T WANT TO LOSE WEIGHT." He says, "EVERYBODY IN AMERICA IS CRAZY." I can't think of an answer to that one.

Everyday he loses at least one thing. If it's a good day, one thing. There are sometimes many things. I try to hear about only one. This morning, I didn't want to hear even one thing, but I didn't get the phone off the hook before he called to tell me he had lost a letter from Wilcox. He said the letter from Wilcox is worth a lot to him. When he told me about the letter—whenever he tells me about any letter he has lost—he uses his old work words, but now all his old work words have a *re* in front of them. *Re*financing. *Re*negotiating. *Re*establishing. (Is adding a *re* to these words another loss?)

Even though I understand all these words, I didn't understand what the letter was about. I never understand any of the letters he says he has lost. I asked him, did he look in mother's desk, in the little cubbies in the top part, where she keeps all the letters and bills. He said, "What?" I said, "MOTHER'S DESK. THE LITTLE CUBBIES." He said, "THIS IS NOT YOUR MOTHER'S LETTER." I said, "Call the lawyer and get him to send you another letter, and he said, "CAN'T." That's the thing about all the things my father loses; once they are gone there is no way for him to get them back, ever.

I didn't get upset about it until yesterday, Sunday, when we were all over there to celebrate his birthday. While everybody was at the dining room table, eating lasagne, I was thinking, *Pretty soon Mother will bring in the cake, and all the children and grandchildren will sing Happy Birthday, and he'll count his candles, and he'll see 71 things that he can't ever get back, ever.* My throat started to feel tight, and then my mother grabbed my elbow and motioned with her head toward the kitchen.

In the kitchen she poured me a glass of water. "Can I give you anything else? An aspirin?"

I said, "No, but do something for Dad. Put just one candle on the cake."

She said, "If I don't put them all on the cake, he'll think we're cheating him. He'll say—"I've lived all those years, I deserve my candles."

I hugged my mother when she said, "I deserve my candles." I don't usually hug her; we stopped that when I was, maybe, 12. I forgot what she felt like close to me. She is smaller than I thought she was, and not as stiff. I keep thinking of her as getting old like my Dad, but she isn't. She's still young and fast. A jogger. She plays tennis and wins.

When we pulled apart, we looked at each other for a few seconds. That was new, too. We don't usually look at each other. It felt right at first, and then we both acted fluttery and tried to find something to do with our hands. She went for the silverware drawer, and I opened a cupboard to look for napkins.

Then she came close to me again and said, almost in a whisper, "Don't let your Daddy know, but he is losing his hearing."

"How come he hasn't told me himself?" I asked.

"He doesn't know," she said.

So then I went back to the dining room to watch him. He was sitting stiff-backed and forward in his chair, what you might call *on the edge of his seat*. His arms were folded tightly across his chest, and his mouth was hanging just a little open. I thought he didn't know his mouth was open. He leaned even more forward and made a noise in the back of his throat, as if he was going to say something, but he didn't. All he did was move his eyes from face to face, back and forth, as if the conversation were a tennis match he was watching. I wondered if he saw winners and losers here, too.

I waved my mother back into the kitchen. She said, "I don't know what to do. He's driving me crazy." Then she got out the cake and handed me three packets of birthday candles. "We might as well give him what he says he wants."

I went ahead and put the candles on the cake. It was a loaf cake and big enough. I lined them up close together. Ten across and seven down. Then added two in the corner. One to wish on.

When Mother carried it in, everyone sang, and then he blew out all the candles in two breaths. He leaned over close to Georgie, my youngest. "Bet you can't do that in two breaths," he said.

Georgie told him he can hold his breath and count to 94. He said he used to only be able to count to 63, but by next summer he'll be able to do 108.

Dad said, "What?"

So first thing this morning, I called my friend, the one who is married to the ear man. She gave me options—hearing aids, surgery, vitamin therapy. She told me names of people to take him to. Then I went to town to check out the hearing aids. I got pamphlets. Brochures. I went to the library to Xerox articles and to find books to give to him. After I spent a couple of hours, I had a bagful of stuff. A hoard of stuff. It was almost too heavy to carry, I had found so much. I decided to celebrate my finds with something chocolate.

That is when I saw my mother with the young man. When I went for the chocolate. I didn't just see her with a young man, I saw her with his arm around her shoulders. He was leaning close to her. He was saying something in her ear. She was laughing. Not like a woman driven crazy. More like a girl on a date. That's what I saw. He was laughing. They were laughing, and they were walking into the chocolate place, that new little place on Pierce Street, the one I told her about. "What a find," I said. "It's darling. For tea in the afternoon. And try their dark chocolate truffles," I said. "You'll die over their dark chocolate truffles."

And there she was, going for one. There was her bright, silver hair, ruffling in the breeze and looking Hollywood. There was the back of her black coat with the belt tied behind. And hanging from her left shoulder, because she is left handed, was her black leather pouch-purse. I thought, *maybe it's not her*. I thought, *maybe it's another thin, silver-haired woman in a black coat with the belt tied behind and a black leather pouch-purse*.

I went up close to the window, but all I could see was him standing in my view of her. And he was plenty to see. Dark-haired, tawny-skinned, with the kind of profile you'd see on the back of a coin. He wore a khaki trench coat and had his belt tied behind, too. Maybe she got the idea from him. He leaned close to her again. Said something in her ear. Touched her arm.

This was not my mother. My mother reads to a blind person every week. She makes lists of things to do and crosses each item off after she does it. She keeps her check book balanced. She's not the kind of person who hugs, and if she did, she would never do it here in town, in front of everyone.

I decided to go in. I thought, if it is her, I'll just say hello, very casually, "Oh, hello, Mother." Then I'll push the bag at her. "Here's the stuff I collected on hearing loss." She'll have to take it. Then I'll walk out. And she'll be *holding the bag*. Ha. The guy with the profile will stand there looking at her *holding the bag* . . . .

I carried the bag to my car, and then I drove over to see my father. He was expecting me, and I didn't want him to count my not showing up as another loss.

When I got there, he didn't answer the doorbell. I waited. Rang again. Again. Then I went around to the back and took the key from under the mat in the garage. "Anybody home?" I called. "Dad?"

I found him in the living room, sitting at my mother's desk. I stood quietly behind the glass doors, at an angle he could not see, and watched him as he pulled envelopes and folded papers out of the cubbies at the top. He took each letter out of its envelope and looked at it for several seconds, then folded it up exactly as it was and put it back. Watching him, I started to sweat in my coat, but didn't dare take it off.

Finally, I called, "Dad?" He didn't look up. I called again. "DAD?"

This time, he jolted out of his chair. "Francie?" he said, "What are you doing here?" He stood up quickly and closed the top of the desk, locked it and put the key in his pocket. Then he made that sound at the back of his throat, as if he was going to say something else, but he didn't.

"We had a date," I said. "Remember?"

"No. But I forget things."

"That's not true. You remember everything you've ever lost."

"Sure, letters, keys, and now it's my mind that's going."

"Don't be silly."

"Your mother's right. I can't remember anything. Can't even find that letter from Wilcox. Did I tell you about refinancing the Wilcox deal?"

"This morning," I said. I put the bag down.

"What do you have there?" he asked.

"Oh, just some books I picked up at the library."

He stepped sideways, first with his right foot, then his left. It was a nervous dance. "Are they good?" he asked.

I said, "I don't know."

"I can't find my library card," he said. "Maybe I could borrow yours. Maybe you could get me some books."

I unbuttoned my coat. I found myself stepping sideways,

too. "Dad," I said. "I've got to talk to you. It's very important."

"What?"

"IT'S VERY IMPORTANT," I shouted. "I HAVE TO TELL YOU SOMETHING."

"WELL, GO AHEAD THEN. I'M LISTENING."

"Let's sit down."

"What?"

"LET'S SIT DOWN. THIS WILL TAKE A WHILE."

"WELL, IF YOU'RE STAYING, WHY DON'T YOU SHED YOUR COAT?"

I took off my coat. I felt shivery after being so hot and sweating for so long. So I put it back on.

"YOU COLD?"

"A LITTLE."

"WELL, IT'S NOT COLD IN HERE. YOU SICK?"

"NO. JUST FEEL KIND OF COZY WITH IT ON."

"IT'S NOT GOOD FOR YOU TO KEEP YOUR COAT ON INSIDE."

I didn't want to say that with my coat on I felt safe, and with it off, I didn't. I didn't want to say anything about how it feels to lose something, even the smallest, most ridiculous kind of thing, even a thing that is too hot, and too heavy, and not even good for you.

"SO WHAT'S THIS IMPORTANT THING YOU WANT TO TALK ABOUT WITH YOUR COAT ON?"

"You're right," I said. "I'll take my coat off. I feel silly." I went to the front hall closet to hang it up and took a long time finding a hanger. I tried to think of something to talk about besides what I already had.

But when I sat down on the couch, across from him, he stood up suddenly and took the cushion off the chair and felt all around the inside edges of the back and the armrests. "I JUST THOUGHT I MIGHT BE ABLE TO FIND THAT LETTER," he said. "I THINK I WAS SITTING IN THIS CHAIR WHEN I HAD IT LAST."

"WELL, YOU SEE YOU'RE NOT CRAZY," I said. "YOU

REMEMBER WHERE YOU WERE SITTING WHEN YOU HAD IT LAST."

"BUT I WAS WRONG. THE LETTER ISN'T HERE." He made that sound again, as if he was going to say something. And then he did. He said, "SO, NOW TELL ME. WHAT IS THIS IMPORTANT THING YOU WANT TO TALK ABOUT?"

"I want to talk to you about Mother," I said.

"What?"

"MOTHER," I said. "I'M WORRIED ABOUT MOTHER."

"OH? WHAT ABOUT MOTHER?"

"I think she's losing her hearing," I said.

"What?"

"SHE'S LOSING HER HEARING."

"NO. SHE'S NOT LOSING HER HEARING."

"SHE'S NOT?"

"NO. I'M THE ONE LOSING HEARING. YOUR MOTHER'S NOT LOSING ANYTHING. SHE'S GETTING THINGS."

"WHAT KIND OF THINGS?" I asked, although I knew that one of them was a dark chocolate truffle and that another was a dark-haired man.

"YOUR MOTHER'S GOT A FELLOW," he said. "HANDSOME YOUNG GUY."

"What?" I asked.

"A FELLOW," he said. "THEY GO OUT AND LOOK AT DOO-DADS TOGETHER. ACCESSORIES, THEY CALL THEM. THEY GO OUT TO FIND ACCESSORIES TOGETHER."

"THAT'S JUST SHOPPING," I said.

"OH, THEY DO MORE THAN SHOP. BELIEVE ME."

"YOU THINK SO?"

"OF COURSE. BUT WHAT DO I KNOW? NOTHING. I CAN'T EVEN FIND THE KEYS TO MY CAR."

"DAD, YOU'RE NOT LOSING YOUR MIND. YOUR MIND IS AS GOOD AS IT EVER WAS."

"NOPE. IT ISN'T. IF IT WAS, I WOULDN'T BE THINKING ALL THE TIME ABOUT YOUR MOTHER BEING WITH

HIM, THAT DECORATOR, AND NOT WITH ME."

I didn't know whether to tell him he hadn't lost his wife or he hadn't lost his mind, so I just sat there, shivering and wishing I had kept my coat.

"WELL, NOW YOU SEE, I'M CRAZY. EVERYONE KNOWS THOSE GUYS ARE ALL HOMOSEXUAL. I'M A NUT TO WORRY," he said.

I picked up the bag with all the books in it, and I put it down on the floor beside his feet. "Why don't you take a look at this material I got for mother. It's about hearing aids."

"What?"

"IT'S ABOUT HEARING AIDS."

He said, "I DON'T WANT TO KNOW ABOUT HEARING AIDS."

"IT'LL HELP YOU," I said.

"NOT A BIT," he said.

"But this is something you've lost that you can get back," I said. "YOU COULD GET IT BACK."

"DON'T WANT IT BACK. DON'T WANT TO HEAR ANYTHING ANY MORE," he said.

"YOU'RE JUST SAYING THAT."

"NOPE."

"But Dad, you could talk to people. You could hear the punch lines to jokes."

"What?"

"YOU COULD HEAR THE PUNCH LINES TO JOKES."

"I'VE ALREADY HEARD EVERYTHING I WANT TO HEAR."

"NO," I said, "THAT IS NOT TRUE. IT'S NOT TRUE."

He looked at me, and I could see by the droop of his shoulders that it was. Everything about him seemed to be falling, his eye lids, his jowls, the corners of his lips.

"YOU'VE GOT TO PULL YOURSELF TOGETHER," I shouted. I felt silly, such a useless thing to say.

He shook his head. "TOO LATE," he shouted back.

I felt myself deflating, too. This was hopeless, the end of the father I had known.

"NO," I said. "Anything is possible. If you think you can, you can." I hadn't shouted, but he nodded solemnly, as if he heard. "IF YOU THINK YOU CAN. IF YOU THINK YOU CAN," I shouted.

I felt like a criminal, a low-down, lousy cheater, giving him a logo from a Disney World sweatshirt, a bumpersticker slogan, the little engine that could. I wanted to say, "I'm sorry." I wanted to do something. "Can I get you anything?" I asked.

He didn't seem to hear. He got up without saying anything and went into the kitchen. I heard the cupboard doors opening and closing. Then he came back with an envelope in his hand.

"HERE IT IS. I FOUND IT. I FOUND THE LETTER." He put it so close to my face that I had to lean back to see it.

"You see?" he said. "You can't let these things get you down."

"You're right," I said.

"And don't you forget it," he said.

"Thank God. You're not losing your mind," I said.

"What?"

"THANK GOD, YOU'RE NOT LOSING YOUR MIND," I said. "YOUR LUCK IS CHANGING."

"CHANGING? NO, I'M NOT CHANGING ANYTHING. I'M GOING TO LEAVE THE WILCOX DEAL JUST AS IT IS. IT'S JUST FINE," he said, and he ripped up the letter and put the pieces in the bag with the material on hearing aids.

"NOW LISTEN, FRANCIE, I DON'T WANT YOU TO WORRY ABOUT ANY OF THE THINGS I'VE BEEN TELLING YOU. THIS WAS BOUND TO HAPPEN. THINGS HAPPEN WHEN YOU GET OLD. NOW, YOU JUST GO PICK UP YOUR KIDS AND MAKE DINNER AND DON'T WORRY."

"What?" I said.

"DON'T WORRY," he said, and he hugged me to say goodbye, and I could feel how thin and fragile he was next to me. How much weight he had lost. How much bulk. How his hug was not as hard and tight and as it used to be. It didn't make me feel warm as it did once. I put my coat on, and it did not make me feel warm, either.

"Now you go ahead," he said. "GO."

So I started to walk out the door, but he called after me.

"I LOST THE KEY TO YOUR MOTHER'S DESK. SHE'LL KILL ME."

I shouted back, "IT'S IN YOUR POCKET, DAD. THE RIGHT HAND POCKET." I turned to see him reach in and pull it out and hold it up and smile.

"DO YOU HAVE YOUR MITTENS?" he called.

I felt inside my pockets. No gloves. So I held up my bare hands. "LOST MY MITTENS," I called back.

"DON'T WORRY," he shouted. "THEY'LL SHOW UP. EVERYTHING ALWAYS SHOWS UP. AND WHEN THEY DO, I WANT YOU TO CALL ME. I WANT TO HEAR."

An Ordinary Ride up an Old Trail

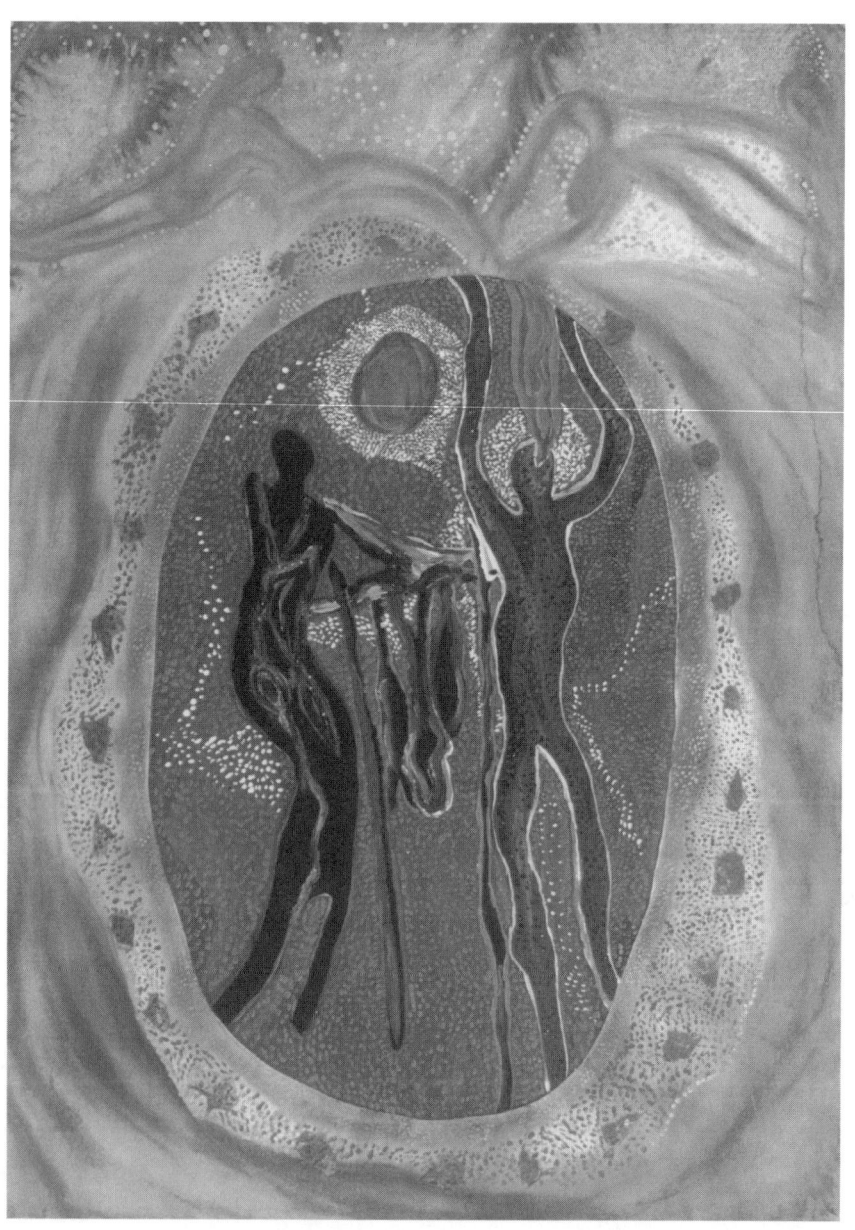

There was a place that had twelve slow horses. They were made to go slow on purpose. And at this place there was a man and a woman on two of these horses that were made to go slow. The man on his slow horse looked at his watch, kept looking at his watch and sighing, as if he was in a hurry. The woman on her slow horse stared off into space and did not seem to notice the man's hurry. The man, who looked as if he was in a hurry, kept saying, "Whoa, boy, whoa, boy," and pulling back on the reins. But the horse was standing still, so it could not stop. Each time the man pulled back on the reins, the horse stepped sideways and backwards. And each time the horse stepped sideways and backwards, the man stiffened his body and made a face of displeasure.

Finally, the woman looked at the man and said, "Why are you in such a hurry to stop? You haven't even started."

The man said, "It's this horse. I'll get another horse, and I'll start over."

The woman said, "That's what you always do. You start over. Why don't you finish something? Why don't you let yourself ride fast for a change? Ride fast all the way to the finish."

But while she was talking, the man was not pulling back on the reins, and the horse started walking slowly on the path that cut across the field and went up the mountain. So, then the woman's horse followed the man's horse.

The woman said, "I'm always following you, even when I know what I'm doing better than you do."

And the man said, "You just think you know what you're doing better than I do. I'm not as slow as you think, and I finish more things than you know about."

And the woman said, "Well, it doesn't matter who knows what, or who is fast, or who is slow, because the horses are going to go where they go with or without us."

The man said, "That's the truth."

The woman said, "And I'll tell you something else. I don't care if we see this mountain or not. I could live my whole life without ever seeing this mountain or any other mountain."

The man said, "That's what's wrong with you. You call everybody too slow, and you blame other people for not finishing things. But you're the one. You're the one who doesn't care if she ever gets to the top."

At the top of the mountain there was a ledge. It was a flat place where benches were pushed against a low stone wall, so that they looked out onto the range of mountains and valleys. And, at the edge of the flat place, there were telescopes bolted to a concrete platform.

The man said, "Here it is. What we've come to see," and he slid off his horse and tied it to a post under a tree.

The woman said, "You go ahead. I'll just wait here," and she made no move to get off her horse.

The man said, "You've got to get off your horse, right now, this minute, and come over here and look at this mountain."

The woman said, "I'm not moving. I can see the mountain from my horse. I don't need to look through a telescope."

The man put a quarter in the telescope, and he looked at the mountain until his quarter ran out, and then he put another quarter in, and another, until finally the woman got off her horse and tied it to a post and went over to stand behind the man. She said, "What's taking you so long?"

He said, "There's a lot to see."

She said, "What do you see?"

He said, "If you take your time, you can see anything."

She said, "What? What do you see?"

He said, "I see rocks. I see grass. I see blades of grass. Over there. You see that mountain over there? Way over there. I can see a blade of grass on that mountain."

The woman laughed. She said, "You're a crazy old guy."

He said, "Not so old."

She said, "Let me see the blade of grass."

He said, "You'll never see it. Even if you look."

She said, "So, it's all a bluff."

The man laughed, Ha, and the woman looked through the telescope. She said, "I can see it. I see the blade of grass."

He said. "I wish you could. But you do everything too fast. You are entirely too fast, and you do too much."

She said, "That's so terrible?"

He said, "Yes, that's so terrible. What's so terrible is that kid, that young colt, the one with the muscles. That's what's so terrible."

The woman turned her face and looked through the telescope, but the quarter had run out. She said, "The quarter's run out. Do you have another one?"

He said, "I've always had everything for you. I've been stuck fast to you, bolted to you, like this telescope here in this cement, but you, you've been galloping off, anywhere, with those young studs. What's wrong with you?"

She said, "I like living fast." She said, "And I'll tell you, there's something about fast that you like or you wouldn't like me the way you do."

The man put his hand in his pocket and jiggled the change. He looked over at the mountain, where he said that he saw the blade of grass, and he said, "Here. Here's a quarter. Would you like to try to see the blade of grass?"

The woman said, "Yes. Yes I would. I've always wanted to see what you see."

The man said, "Take your time. Those horses there aren't in any hurry to get back."

She said, "They're so slow. They might not even get back."

He said, "That was my line."

His Mother's Piano

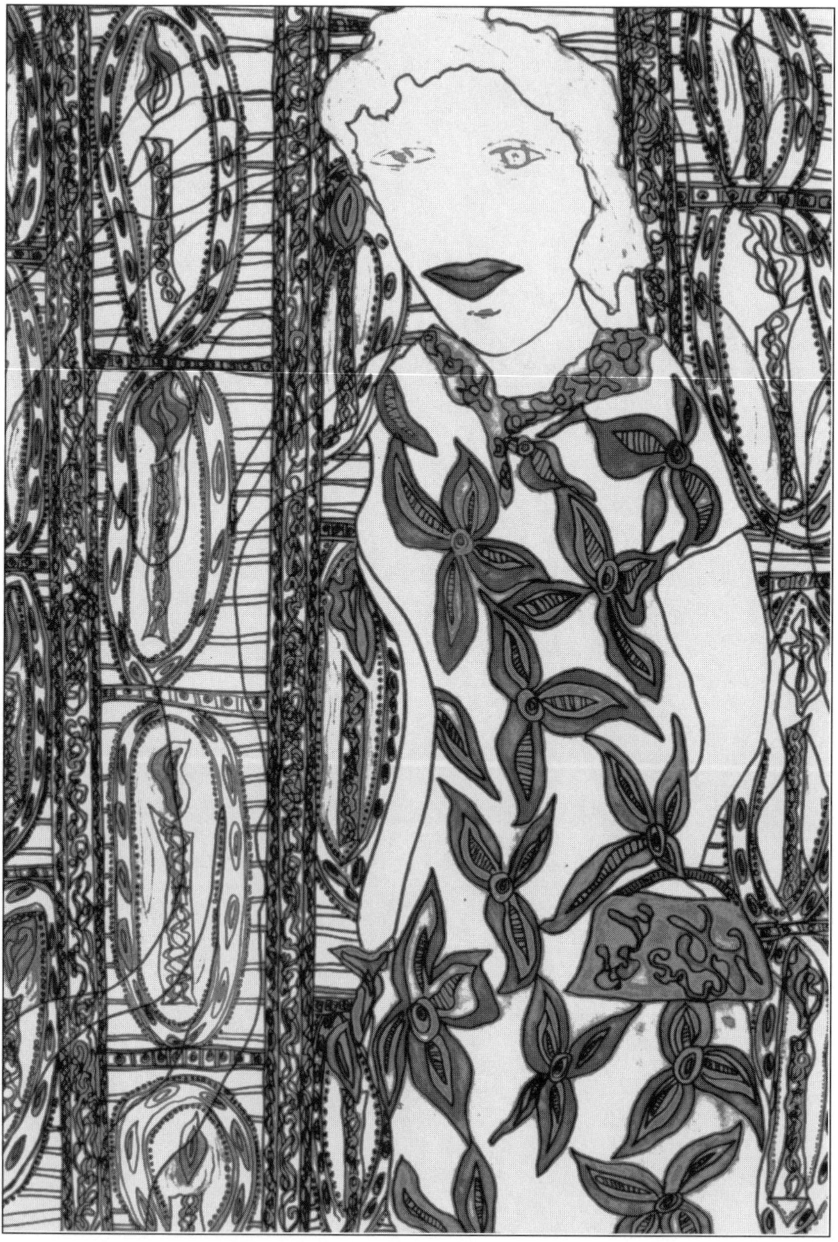

He had a maid who could play the piano. Her name was Requel. Requel played the same pieces on the piano that his mother had played. His mother had played "Jesus Loves Me, This I Know." His mother had played "God Bless America." But when his mother's fingers got bad, she said, "I don't want to see this piano in my house anymore." She said, "You'll have to keep it in your house." He told his mother he couldn't keep the piano in his house, either.

He said, "I don't even know how to play 'Chop Sticks.'" He said, "I don't know anyone who does."

His mother said, "But you could meet someone."

So he moved the couch and two chairs out of his living room and moved the piano to the place where the couch and two chairs had been. Then there was nothing in the living room for anyone to sit on except the piano bench. But the friends who came to his house and stood around the piano said they liked the piano in his living room. They said they liked the piano better than they liked the couch and the two chairs. They said all the piano needs is things, and they gave him things to put on top of his piano. They gave him things they said they thought seemed right for the top of a piano, things that needed to be dusted or polished. They gave him brass candlesticks, silver picture frames, and ivory elephants.

So then he found Requel. Requel dusted the piano, and she dusted the things on top of the piano, and then she played her pieces on it every day. "I am so lucky to do this," she said. "To play this piano. Do you know what? Do you know what I am going to do?"

He said, "No. What are you going to do, Requel?"

She said, "When I get some money, I'm going to study the piano. God wants me to."

After that, she played the piano every day. She played the piano before she dusted instead of after. Then she played the piano instead of dusting it. She said God was listening.

He said, "Requel, God is watching." He said, "Requel, God wants the piano dusted and polished." He said, "Use that special oil my mother used to use. It's in the gold bottle."

Requel said, "Okay, I do it."

He said, "Be sure to polish all the things on top of the piano. God wants everything nice and shiny."

Requel said, "Okay, I do it."

He said, "God and my mother, Requel. My mother is coming on Thursday. Please have it dusted by Thursday."

Requel said, "Don't you worry. I do it."

He said, "Requel, if my mother sees her piano looking the way it does, she'll get upset." He said, "Requel, if my mother gets upset, God will get upset."

Requel said, "Don't you worry. I do it."

He could see from the hallway that the piano looked as dull as it had looked the day before. He could see that the candlesticks, the picture frames, and the elephants all looked as dull as they had looked the day before. But Requel! He saw that Requel looked different. Her cheeks were pink, and her lips were pink, and on her eyelids was something dark and glistening. Then he saw it was not just her face she had polished. She had brushed back her hair and changed her clothes. She had changed out of her worn jeans and into her black dress. She had even changed the piece she played on the piano. She was playing "He's Got the Whole World in His Hands." She was playing it very slowly. When she finished playing, she smiled at him.

"Don't you worry," she said. "I do everything."

He said, "Not everything, Requel."

She said, "The polishing, it is easy. Tomorrow I do the easy. Tomorrow I polish."

Requel sat on the bench in front of the piano, and his mother stood beside the piano. His mother held, in one hand, the gold bottle, and in the other, a white cloth.

He said, "But mother, your fingers."

His mother said, "They're fine, today, but my piano. Look at my piano."

He said, "It's just a little dust."

His mother said, "It's a sin."

He looked at the piano, but he saw that his mother looked at Requel. So he looked at Requel. She had on her shining face and her black dress.

His mother said, "A girl like this. She can't stay with you another day."

He said, "What?"

His mother said, "She's coming home with me." His mother said, "I'm taking the piano, too."

He said, "What?"

His mother said, "Requel can play her songs for God. And I will listen."

Last Chance Louie

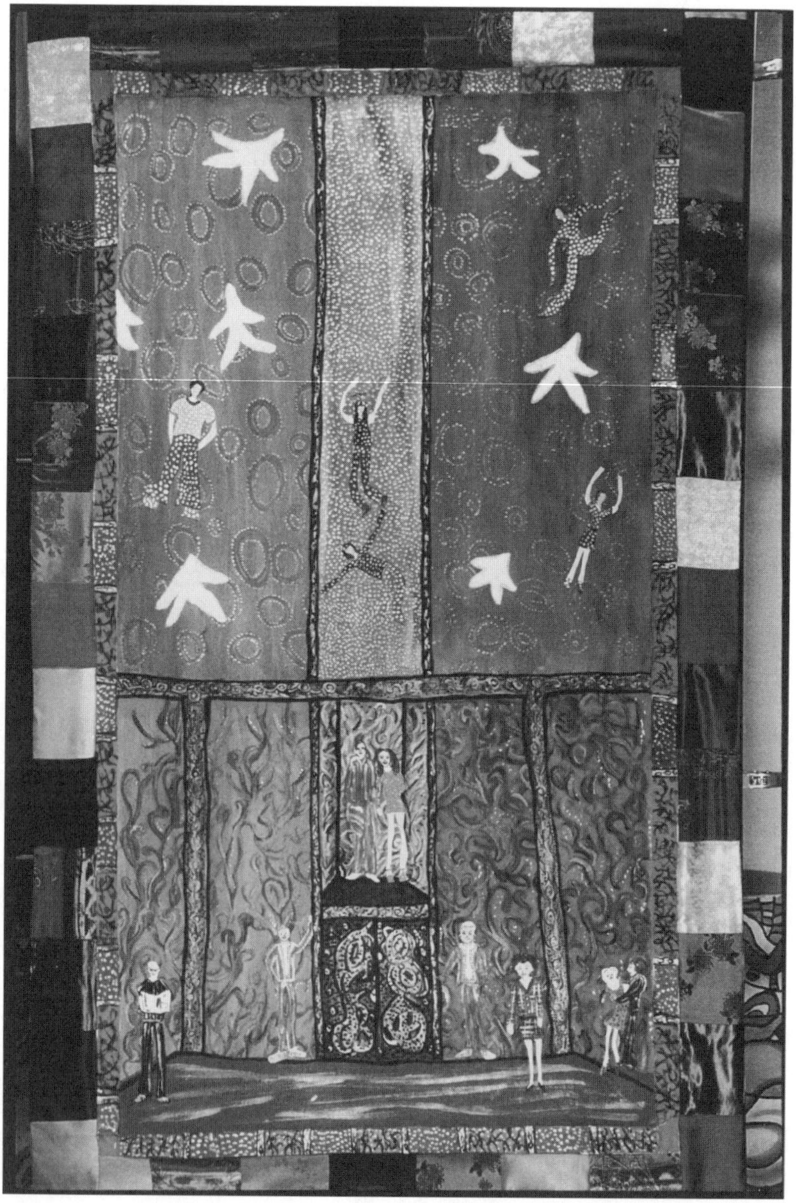

Uncle Will never traveled with Aunt Molly. Whenever she asked him if he wanted to, he always said, "No thanks, I'll read about it in *The National Geographic.*" So she climbed mountains in India and explored ruins in Mexico by herself.

Finally, he offered to move all of his enterprises and his entire household to the other end of America, from Michigan to California, which was as far as he would go. No one knows the reason why, but one of the aunts said he thought if Aunt Molly could see an ocean, as she drove to the grocery store, she would feel closer to whatever it was she was looking for, and she would stay home more often.

"Ninety-six countries is enough countries," Uncle Will said.

Aunt Molly was trying for one hundred, but agreed to settle in for a while, if she could have a house on a hill with a garden, and a music room with tall windows to look out of while she played her piano. That was her other love—after traveling and Uncle Will, and her two sons and one daughter (who were mostly grown)—she loved music. It was the only thing she had ever loved that she felt she had not loved well enough.

"I'm just not very good, you know," she'd say.

Her friends and relatives always told her she was, and nobody lied, because they weren't expecting to hear a genius, but she was expecting to be one.

With that in mind, she told the realtor not to take her to any house unless it had a splendid room for her piano.

The first house they saw belonged to Anita Stewart, who Aunt Molly remembered and loved from the days when she was a very little girl and her Grandpa Saltzman used to take her on Saturdays to the movies at the Orpheus. Back then, the movies were silent and Anita Stewart was a big star.

The year Aunt Molly went to her house, 1955, Ms. Stewart was very, very thin and pale and wore thick powder on her face and many shawls. Still, it was a thrill to meet her, even though the house was nothing much. "A bastard, white colonial," Aunt Molly called it. Everything about it seemed dry to her and cracked and peeling. Even the garden, which climbed a hill in layers like steps, offered little.

But the piano was something wonderful. Aunt Molly stood looking at it for a long time, studying the odd sheets of peculiar notations—resembling mathematical equations or scientific formulas—that rested on the music stand. There were boxes and boxes of the sheets, all with the same odd markings, stacked on a side table.

"What's this?" Aunt Molly asked Ms. Stewart, who was following them through the house, talking to them, as if they were guests.

"Oh, those," Ms. Stewart said. "Those are from Last Chance Louie. Everybody knows about *him*."

Aunt Molly glanced again at the sheets. "But is this music?" she asked.

"You're looking at *A Foggy Day*. Here. *Here's Fools Rush In, I Only Have Eyes For You, Unforgettable . . . .*"

"Oh, My. *Unforgettable . . . .*" Aunt Molly was ignited. She could not have been more excited at an archaeological dig in China.

"I've always wanted . . . ," she said.

Ms. Stewart sat down on the piano bench, arranged all of her skirts and shawls, and played *Unforgettable* with such confidence, such frills, such flair, that Aunt Molly sat down on the couch.

"I have no ability what-so-ever," Ms. Stewart said when she was finished. "This is all because of Last Chance Louie."

Poor Aunt Molly. She nearly fainted from desire.

"Where is this man?" she asked, almost in a whisper.

"Oh, dear. I haven't seen him in a while. He might be retired now. He always wanted to travel. And God knows, he deserves to. He's been nursing the hopeless for years . . .,"

Ms. Stewart's voice trailed off and she began to play *Misty*.

When she was finished, the two women talked music for some time, and Ms. Stewart played two more songs: *The Best Things in Life are Free* and *April Showers*.

Before she left the house, Aunt Molly got Last Chance Louie's phone number from Ms. Stewart, who told her, "This might not be a working number. He might have moved."

He had. The number was disconnected, and Aunt Molly didn't know anybody who knew anybody in town, except the realtor, who got on it immediately, but Last Chance Louie had had his troubles: a house fire, a broken foot, a move. He was hard to track down. Finally the realtor looked in the phone book under Last Chance, and there he was.

"I don't have any talent," she told him, when she finally reached him and explained how she heard of him. "I don't even have a piano. All I have is love."

He agreed to meet her right away and get her started. He even borrowed a piano for her to use—from his old friend, Anita Stewart, it turned out. Ms. Stewart, who was happy to have the company, said they could come every Monday until her house was sold.

So, each Monday Last Chance would limp into the music room, brandishing the cane he never used for walking. "I don't need this old thing," he said. It was a really handsome one with a carved ivory handle in the shape of a serpent. "I just carry it because a friend brought it back from somewhere for me, and I don't want to hurt her feelings." He would frown when he said it, but he was always frowning; not that he had a case against anybody or anything, but because he seemed to have that kind of face, heavy jowled with a wide mouth that appears to have to work hard to get a smile up.

So frowning and limping, and without taking off his cap (he never did that), he sat down on the piano bench each Monday at ten o'clock and began to play whatever song, or two or three songs, he was going to teach her that day— *Paper Moon, It's Delovely, Magic is the Moonlight*.

Poor Aunt Molly. This is all she wanted now: To do what Louie did.

"Like this," he would say. He had a voice that was as dark and rich as black coffee and fingers that knew how to love the keys.

"I'll teach you," he promised, and he did. Each week, after he had played his two or three pieces, he would write his notations—letters and numbers and arrows—on unlined sheets and put the sheets in big notebooks. He showed her what all his scribblings meant, how they represented chords, or broken chords, or petatonic scales. He showed her how to put the chords and scales together with connectors and fill-ins. He showed her how to use pentatonic scales with augmented chords. He gave her what he called hints. (You can always add a 6th to a major.)

All the tricks he had ever learned or invented, and that was plenty of tricks, he taught to Aunt Molly.

In the meantime, she could not find a house that she liked, so she bought Anita Stewart's house. It was not the house she dreamed of, but she was used to it. She put her own piano in the music room and added flowers to the garden.

Last Chance kept on coming to her music room and filled a whole notebook with songs. A year passed. Two more notebooks. Another year. Another notebook. Her sons got married. Her daughter began to travel around the world. Two more notebooks. The first grandchild was born. Aunt Molly played her pieces every day no matter what else she had to do and was as happy as she had ever been anywhere in the world. She neglected to go anyplace else. Never even mentioned a trip. Uncle Will counted his blessings.

But then one day Aunt Molly realized she wanted to learn something more. "I want to do what Louie does," she told Uncle Will. "I want to arrange the songs myself. I don't want Louie to do it. I want to do it. I want to decide what chords, what connectors, what fill-ins, what trills. I would be the happiest woman in the world if I could do that."

Last Chance Louie was willing. In fact, he was heroic. He tried a dozen ways to show her. He explained everything carefully. He drew diagrams. He played for her. He teased her, yelled at her, begged her. He brought flash cards, tapes, a bulletin board with chords represented by pieces of felt in different colors. But whatever he did, even Last Chance could not teach her; she could learn to play whatever he arranged, but she could not learn to arrange.

This was the first thing that Aunt Molly had ever decided to do that she could not do. It was devastating. She tried harder. But, to put it nicely, the music that she made did not fill the house with gladness. Uncle Will complained. Her sons and daughters-in-law complained. She redoubled her efforts, and spent longer and longer hours arranging and rearranging the songs. The results were no better.

But Aunt Molly would not give up. She spoke to God and promised Him anything if He would help her. When she'd done it, she would look for a sign from Him letting her know what she was to do for Him. It didn't matter what; she would do it.

Not long after that, Last Chance came into her music room and took off his hat. He put it on a table, and did not sit down right away. Aunt Molly knew something was up.

"What's wrong?" she asked him, thinking it was a family problem, or his health, or his finances . . . .

"Look," he said. "I can't teach you anymore. I've taught you everything I know. I haven't got anything more to teach."

Aunt Molly never did take no easily, and besides she had made a deal with God. "Louie," she said. "You are the most magnificent, talented, generous person, I've ever met."

Louie, even though it appeared to be difficult for his particular mouth, smiled. He knew Aunt Molly and might have guessed what was coming.

"Louie, sometimes I think you are too generous. You give your talent away."

Louie shook his head. There was a flat spot on the right side where he usually kept his hat.

"You should charge more. I'm going to be the first student to raise your price, and you deserve it."

"No," he said. "I can't take your money."

"Louie. I know it has been hard lately, trying to teach me to arrange. But why don't we stop that for now. We'll go back to just playing. I can play."

"You don't understand. You have all of my pieces. You have over three hundred songs."

"So you'll arrange new songs," she said, and she waved the problem aside with a flick of her wrist.

"No," he said. "There aren't any more songs."

"That's impossible," she said. "I'll find you more. The world always has songs."

He shook his head. "A person has to move on."

"You're tired of me and angry, because I can't learn to arrange. But I will. I will."

"No," he said. "I just don't have anything more to offer you. There isn't anything more."

"Of course there is. You are a genius. You are the *Last Chance*. There must be more."

Louie shook his head.

So Aunt Molly got out Uncle Will's brandy and offered him a drink. "Here's to us," she said.

He smiled. "Here's to moving on," he said.

"But Louie," she said. "I've loved every minute of my years with you. I've loved every piece, every note I've played. I've loved you."

"Then you don't need me anymore," he said, and he walked out of the door.

Poor Aunt Molly. She could not believe her Last Chance was gone. She tried to call him a few times, but he didn't answer. She heard from Anita Stewart, who still came by to say hello and see the old house, that he'd gone to Europe, and then, from someone else, that he was in Sun Valley.

Aunt Molly stopped playing the piano. She stopped seeing the new friends she had made. She stopped writing to her relatives.

Uncle Will began to worry, until she decided to take a trip.

"I need to go somewhere," she said.

He said "Sure" when she said "Tahiti," and off she went with one bag, as usual.

When she came home, she had two bags, one of them filled with Tahitian prayer boxes, wooden bowls, beaded belts, and gauzy wedding dresses.

She put the prayer boxes and bowls on the side table in the music room and hung the belts and the dresses on the wall, the way you'd hang a painting. She liked the way they fit in, as if they belonged. Even Uncle Will agreed.

"I want to look at them," Aunt Molly told him, "And remember all the stories about the people I met when I found them. That is what I love. The stories about the people. I like to know how they live . . . how they cook their meals . . . and do their laundry . . . how they build their houses and pray to their Gods . . . how they marry and bury."

She told him all the stories. Then she sat down at her piano. "But I missed my music." She got a dreamy look in her eyes and began to play "Somebody Loves Me."

"You know," she said when she was finished, "Louie was right. I'll never do what Louie does. I'll never be George Gershwin. I'll never be Irving Berlin or Johnny Mercer. But I can play," and with a side-long glance at Uncle Will, and a quick toss of her head, she played "Coquette," her eyes flashing all the while.

"I love my music," she said.

And from that moment on, even when she grew old and sick and could not leave her home, Aunt Molly played the three hundred songs that Last Chance had given her, over and over—four or five songs every single day.

Howie the Bum

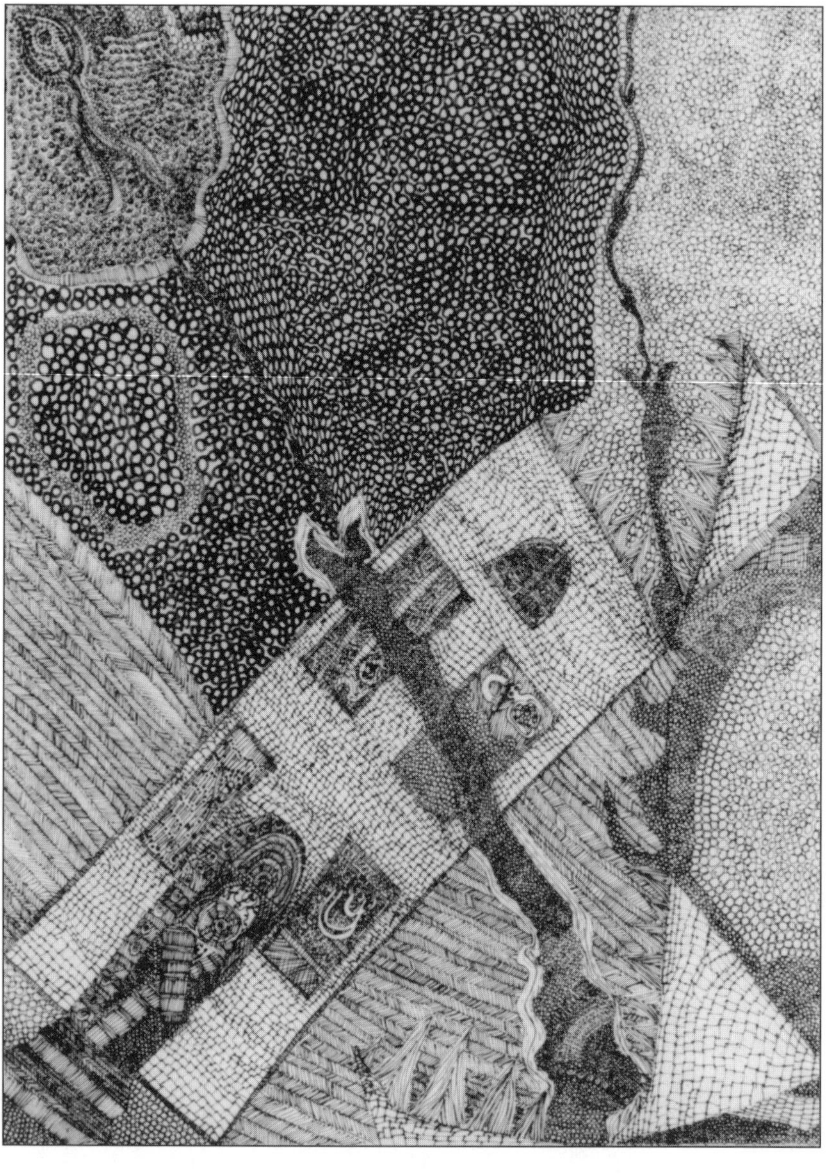

"Howie is a bum," his father said. "That's what he is, and that's all he's ever going to be." This was nothing he had not said before.

He went up to Howie's room, which was a mess as usual—with books strewn everywhere, their pages bent and stained, their spines pulled apart. It made him furious to see Howie treat books like that. "He likes to read them so much, why can't he put them away?" he shouted. "And look at this?" He pointed at the floor. There were half-eaten, hard-as-rocks cheeseburgers, jelly donuts, and bagels you could use to break a window. His father stooped to pick up a nearly empty bag of stale potato chips and an upended Coke bottle. It drove him crazy to have such a heap of garbage in his house. On top of it all were crumpled t-shirts and dirty jeans. "These things cost money, and now look at them."

And where was Howie? On his bed, tangled in sheets that were pulled so far out of place, the blue damask print of the mattress could be seen.

"What are you reading?" his father asked, but Howie hardly grunted an acknowledgement. He was too engrossed.

His father shook his head and frowned, as he told all the relatives, "I would be pleased. I would be thrilled, but Howie was reading a book for a course he flunked two years ago. Sometimes he even reads books for a class he has refused to take."

The aunts—Evelyne, and Rose, and Winnie, and Iris—all told him boys take longer to grow up, and not to worry.

"Howie just can't do what he's supposed to do when he's supposed to do it," he said. "I don't think he ever will." His father grabbed at his hair, as if he was pulling it out. "You see? You see what that boy is doing to me? I'll be bald in a year."

"Relax. Give him some time. He'll go back to college, just like he did before, and he'll grow up like everybody does," Aunt Iris said.

"He's just acting like this, because of the times. There are a lot of boys doing just what Howie is doing," Aunt Winnie said.

This was back in the 70's, and some of the neighbors were complaining about their sons, who had also dropped out of school or grown their hair long enough to pull back in a ponytail, but this did not give comfort to Howie's father. He had started wearing hats to cover his bald spot and told Howie it was because of him that he needed to. Howie shrugged and went back to his books, which aggravated his father even more.

But then, all at once, in the dreary cold of a damp February, Howie started doing what he was supposed to do. He woke up in the morning. He got dressed. He filled out forms and mailed applications. He even returned his overdue library books.

His father stopped pulling out his hair, and the whole family—aunts, uncles, a few of the cousins—sighed in collective relief. Howie kept it up for months. It was a miracle.

Then one sunny day early in September, he came to the breakfast table. "Mom, Dad, I've had enough of this shit," he said, and he set out to be what his father had always said he was. A bum.

All that he took was $30.00 in cash, his driver's license, his social security card, and a grocery bag that held a change of underwear, a tube of Colgate toothpaste, and his red toothbrush. He grabbed an extra t-shirt and a denim jacket, but decided against the extra things. He wanted to travel light.

He folded his grocery bag into a flat little package, said goodbye to all the four bedroom colonials with painted shutters, and trimmed shrubs, and geraniums in pots on front porches, and got in his friend Jimmy Bernstein's old blue Mustang. Jimmy drove him to the corner of Eight Mile and

Woodward, "on the edge of Detroit," as Howie used to put it, and there he stood with his bag in his hand and his thumb out.

He had a certain neighborhood in mind, and he got himself a ride straight to the street three blocks east of the Goodrich Tire sign, where he once saw some old men sitting on benches in front of a grocery store. He thought this looked like a place a person could live.

The grocery store was gone, but it didn't bother him. He stood on the corner with his hands in his pockets, just breathing deeply. The air smelled good. A soft breeze carried a hint of earth and leaves, and there was the constant swell of heat, thick and heavy like a blanket that brought rich, meaty odors from Anthony's Bar and Grill in the middle of the block.

Every so often, a bus screeched to a halt in front of him and blasted the street with a gaseous burp of oily fumes. Howie loved buses. He loved the smell of them, the sound of them. He liked watching all the people getting off and getting on. A thin woman in a tight red dress, a black purse banging against her hip as she ran to catch the bus, shouting, "Wait," an old man in a blue grey cardigan, shuffling slowly, as if his battery was running down, a fat black woman with a grocery bag like his, only fuller—who were all these people? Where were they going? What were they leaving?

Standing on the corner, inhaling the promise of it all, Howie knew this was it, heaven. No more hassling. *You're too late, you're too different, too smart, too dumb, difficult, lazy, wrong.* This was freedom from all that. This was his piece of the American pie.

He looked around. Besides Anthony's Bar and Grill, there was Our Lady of Refuge Catholic Church on the corner, and beside the parking lot, a strip of stores: We Care Cleaners—in by ten out by five; Instant Cash—Buy, Sell, Trade—Shotguns, Rifles, Cameras, T.V.'s, Stereo's, Lawn Mowers, Snow Blowers, Bikes, Musical Instruments; and a Body Art Studio—Fine Line Quality Work by Doctor John.

Grime coated the windows of buildings, paint flaked off woodwork, papers littered the sidewalks. He liked that. He liked the way everything was the color of dust. This was the place Howie had been looking for all his life. Everything a guy could need and nobody to get too close or ask too much.

He could see how true that was when he looked across the street. He saw a man shaking all over, making slow progress and talking to himself. A young woman pushing a baby in a stroller didn't look at him, didn't even turn her head, as she passed. Howie watched her. She had the kind of body he liked—ample, with big breasts and a big behind. She walked slowly. She didn't notice Howie. See? My kind of place, Howie thought. Nobody cares who you are.

"Hey, buddy, you new?" It was a tall guy, thin and lanky with a pale, boney face. He stood poised with his back foot ready, heel off the ground, toe dug in for a take off, as if he wanted to step away fast.

"Yeah," Howie said.

"You don't wanna be standing here. The guy owns that cleaners, there, he don't like loitering. He calls the police, alla time. They'll give you shit, man."

Howie nodded. "Thanks," he said. He figured the guy for a kindred spirit. One of *us*, against all of *them*.

"The place to go is that way," the tall guy said, pointing south with his thumb. "A few blocks down. And over one."

He was in a hurry to move on, but Howie wasn't. He just stood there breathing deeply and feeling happier and happier.

Then a police car came by, moving slowly and quietly, like a black shark in dark water. It stopped in front of him.

"You new here?" the cop asked him.

Howie shook his head. "Just passing through," he said. "I'm about to leave."

"Good. Keep on going," the cop said. "We'll be watching for you."

Howie nodded. He figured there was somebody to bug you wherever you went, and he should have been expecting it. He started walking in the direction the tall guy had pointed. He walked for several blocks, noticing signs on all the stores and windows: The Renaissance Party Shoppe: Beer and Wine, Groceries; The Iglesia de Dios Penaecostal Church—on a cement block building painted rose pink; The Convenience Deli: Fresh donuts. Low Prices. Money Orders. We Accept Food Stamps. On a corner, a four-story dark brick building: Sleep Five Dollars. He looked up to see a pale man with sparse hair leaning out of a half-open window, a yellowed shade pulled to the opening. He was smoking a cigar. Next door to that, a storefront boarded up: Condemned. Next door to that, House of Divine Light; Carl's Party Store; Tabernacle of the Holy Spirit; Vacuum Sales; McQuires Printing; Monument to Faith.

He realized he was hungry and thought of going back to Anthony's Bar and Grill. Then he saw The Blue Moon. He stood in front of it. It smelled like french fries. A large white sign in the window spelled out in blue letters: SPECIALS. He didn't bother to read the specials. I'll eat once in a Blue Moon, he thought, and he went in.

A lone customer was sitting at the counter, reading a paper and smoking a cigarette. He looked, to Howie, like a man who had once been very handsome. He was still distinguished-looking with strong bones, a head full of pure white hair, and weathered, ruddy skin. He wore a dark suit, but it was chalky and wrinkled, and not quite the right size—a little short in the pants and long in the sleeves. He had a bottle in a paper bag on his lap, and every so often he'd take a swig.

The man behind the counter, dark-haired and swarthy, in a white shirt unbuttoned enough to show a tuft of chest hair, was cooking up a burger. He waved his spatula at the old guy. "Hey, Sam, you want cheese on this?" he shouted. He had an accent Howie couldn't place.

"No, thank you, Al, just the fries and slaw." He slapped a five on the counter and took another swig. Then he looked up and stared at Howie.

"Haven't seen you before," he said.

Howie nodded. "I'm new in town," he said.

"I used to be new," he said. "I was young. I was everything, then."

"Sam used to be a hot-shot lawyer. Big corporate giant," Al said. It sounded to Howie like he was bragging about someone in his own family.

Howie smiled. "My name is Ace," he said. Nobody had ever called him Ace before, but he liked it. "I came in from Cincinnati." He could be anybody from anywhere.

"Hey," Sam said, "Cincinnati?"

"Yeah. Came to see a friend," Howie said.

Sam smiled. "That's good. Ace...Ace, you play cards?"

"Some," Howie said.

"You play cards, and you'll always have a place to sleep. Take my word for it. Cards is the answer," Sam said.

"Yeah?" Howie said. He hadn't done much card playing, never liked it, never liked the guys who did. Norm Katzman, a guy with greasy hair and pudgy fingers, used to have a gang that played cards—Arnie Keller, Steve Walker, Jimmie Schwartz, Dave Soloman—all those guys were slick. Some of them were nasty. Cheaters. But that was a long time ago, and Howie thought he might think differently now. He might know how to play their game.

"I play cards," Sam said. "I'm a gambling man." He took another swig of his drink. "I was the best. You know why? Pressure. I can take pressure. The higher the stakes, the better I am." He took another swig. He leaned his head back and drank. Howie could see his nose hair and the white stubble on his purplish chin. "I can bluff," Sam said. "You bluff?"

Howie nodded. "Sometimes," he said. He ordered a burger with onions, fries, and slaw, $ 2.75. *A fifty cent tip, $26.75 left*.

"If you're on a roll, you can stay at the place on the corner up there. Can't remember the name. I don't think it has a name. No name. Stay at The No Name. Good clean rooms. Five bucks a night. Not bad."

Howie nodded.

"But be careful. The high rollers are the first to get rolled. Remember that. Watch your pockets. Look behind you. Don't own too much. There's the problem in life. Owning too much. I'm telling you, kid. You get too many things, everybody wants 'em. You own nothin', nobody can take it away."

Howie nodded. "Where do you play around here?"

"Al's place. Three blocks down. On the west side of the street. You go in there, and you go to the back room, and you ask for Red. Tell him Uncle Sam sent you."

Howie went to the place with no name. He got himself a room. It had a bed, a pillow, a rickety table with one drawer that stuck, and no phone. The window was dark with soot and didn't open, and the room smelled of mold and stale cigarettes, but it was a place to leave his bag. He thought it was the bag that made him look like a greenhorn. He checked to make sure his money and his I.D. were still in his back pocket, ran his fingers though his hair, brushed his teeth and went out to find a place to hang around.

He walked for a while. It was the kind of warm evening that reminded him of something pleasant from his childhood, but he wasn't sure what, maybe twilight baseball games or barbeques in the backyard. Back then, sometime long ago, he remembered there was this kind of sky—still fairly light, almost pearl grey, with a waning moon. The moon looked to him like a piece of white jewelry, a mother-of-pearl pendant he'd once given to a girl he'd liked. The girl had given him the shaft, but it raised his spirits to see her necklace in the sky, and he turned the corner.

He found he was standing in front of Al's place. An A, an L and an E were missing from the sign, so at first it looked like L's PAC. L's PAC didn't have a window, but it had a maroon and tan canopy that had been knocked crooked. Howie thought he'd take a look. Why not?

Inside it was smokey, and he liked the way everybody looked—loose and rumpled with long hair and beards. He liked the way guys were sitting with a foot up on a chair, or an elbow on the table. This whole place is full of my own kind, he thought.

He ordered a beer. Then he saw two men walking toward a back room, and he followed them to see what he could. He wasn't going to play, just watch, so he stood by the door with his hands in his pockets and leaned against the wall. He couldn't see much. The room was dark with rough textured paneling on the walls and worn, damp wood on the floor. It smelled like beer and wet wool. Besides the round table, where the men played poker without talking, there was a coat rack loaded with jackets and a small wooden table. There was a bottle of Ripple, a can of Strohs, and a bowl of pistachio nuts on the table. Howie longed to try the Ripple. He longed to grab a handful of pistachio nuts. He wanted to get in the game. He thought he knew enough, but he didn't think he should rush into it. After a minute or two, one of the guys looked at him.

"You a cop?" he asked.

Howie shook his head. Then one guy got up from the table, and the dealer ran his eyes up and down Howie, checking him out.

Howie let him take his look and then, finally, he said, "You Red?"

The guy shook his head. "Moe. I'm Moe." He was tall with a long face, smooth dark hair, and was dressed in black. He reminded Howie of a Doberman pinscher.

"I'm Red," the guy sitting next to Moe said. He had pale, sandy-colored hair that Howie thought must have once been the color of his name.

"Uncle Sam told me to come by. Told me to tell you he's the one who sent me," Howie said.

Red nodded. "Five card draw," he said. "Guts to open. You got any guts?"

Howie felt a stab of fear, like heartburn. He sat down in the empty chair beside Moe and watched him deal. Moe was fast with the cards.

"I bet five," Red said and shoved his chips on the table. He looked to his left. "Eagle?"

Eagle was bald and had a nose like a beak. "Call," Eagle said.

"Topper?" Moe said.

"Same for me." Topper said. He was broad-shouldered and had a cropped haircut that made his head look flat.

Howie glanced at his cards. "I'll call," he said.

Moe nodded. "Cards?" he said.

"Two," Red said.

"Three," Eagle said.

"Topper?" Moe said.

"Two," Topper said.

They all looked at Howie. Howie started feeling prickly. The bottoms of his feet itched. He looked up at the light bulb. A dark green metal shade did nothing to cut the white glare.

Moe cleared his throat.

"None," Howie said.

"I'll take three," Moe said. He looked to his left. "Red, you opened. It's your bet."

"Check," Red said. Then Eagle passed, and Topper passed.

They looked at Howie again.

"I bet twenty dollars," Howie said.

"I fold, " Moe said, and slapped his cards down.

Then Red and Eagle and Topper all folded.

"I call," Topper said. "Whatcha got?"

"A Flush." Howie said, as he fanned his cards out on the table. He had a two, a five, a ten, a jack and a king of hearts. Then he pulled in his chips. He thought of Norm Katzman. He wondered if those guys still played, and if they did, where?

Red threw his ante in the pot and dealt the next hand. "Your turn," he said to Eagle. Eagle didn't look up. "I pass," he said. Then Topper passed. It came to Howie's turn. He had nothing. He didn't have a pair. "I pass," he said. Moe opened at two. Then Red called, and everybody folded. The next hand was the same thing. Not much happening.

"Cards are cold tonight," Moe said. "Looks like we're just playin' for the ante."

Then Topper dealt. Howie looked at his cards. *What's this?* he thought. Another hand with nothing. Not a pair. His high card was a ten. *Are these guys cheating?* he wondered. When it came to his turn, he thought of passing, but then he thought, what the hell. The name of this game is guts. Right? High stakes. Right?

"I bet twenty dollars," Howie said. He said it the same way he would say it if he had a hand like his first one.

Red, Eagle, and Topper folded.

"Your turn Moe," Red said. "What do you do?"

"I'll see your bet and raise you twenty dollars," Moe said.

"Cards?" Red said.

"Two," Moe said.

Howie looked again at his cards. "Three," he said. He drew a deuce, an eight, and an ace, and that gave him two pairs. You see, he thought, life is good. Luck is with me.

"I'll raise you twenty," Howie said.

"I'll call," Moe said.

Howie slapped his cards on the table. "Aces and eights," he said.

"Dead Man's hand," Topper said.

Howie didn't like the sound of his voice. What did he mean Dead Man?

"Three cowboys," Moe said and laid his kings on the table.

Howie felt in his back pocket for the money he didn't have there, then he looked around the table. He smiled, first at Moe, then Red, then Eagle, then Topper. What's the matter here, he thought. These were his kind of guys, but they weren't laughing. He thought, now what? "I have to go to the john," he said. "I'll be back."

"No problem," Moe said. "I'll show you where it's at."

So Howie followed Moe to the men's room. He thought, *This is it. The end.* He didn't look to the left or the right; he didn't fidget or fuss or whine. He went straight to the urinal. What he didn't see was the big guy with the bland face, who was following him. Moe noticed him right away, and as soon as the big guy walked into the men's room, he turned to watch him carefully.

"Whatchu staring at?" the big guy asked.

"Nothin'," Moe said. "Nothin' at all."

"I don't like people starin' at me," the big guy said. He moved real close. He stuck his face in Moe's face.

"I wasn't staring," Moe said. He stepped back, but the guy stayed on him.

"Well, then stop," the big guy said.

"I can't stop what I'm not doing," Moe said. He was backed to the wall. "Cut the crap, Duke."

"I DON'T LIKE PEOPLE STARIN' AT ME," Duke shouted. "DON'T EVER STARE AT ME." He spread his arms and moved closer, so Moe's body was plastered to the wall.

"FOR CHRIST'S SAKE, CUT IT OUT," Moe shouted.

Duke didn't seem to hear him. He had his face nearly touching Moe's face.

"Do you want to stay and watch the games? If you keep this up, we won't let you watch again. That's it. Never again," Moe said. He was speaking very softly.

"I SAID MIND YOUR OWN BUSINESS, YOU SLIMY PIECE OF SHIT, YOU SCUM BAG, YOU ARE A TURD, A FUCKIN' PIG...."

Howie stepped as quickly and quietly as a cat out of the men's room, crept down a short, narrow hall and then out of the back door into the alley. As soon as his feet touched the cement, he took off. He ran as fast as he had ever run, back to his room at the place with no name.

His bag was gone. Now, not only was he without money, he was without underwear and toothpaste. All he had was the shirt on his back, that's it. Nothing. Zippo. Now he was a real bum, not a greenhorn.

The next morning he woke up hungry and thirsty. He walked aimlessly, trying to decide what to do. He was headed for the business district. Each time he passed a restaurant—Don's Coney Island, The Blue Moon, Joy Garden, The Flaming

Embers, Rita's, The Lafayette Cafe, Gus's Deli—he felt his back pocket, as if the money might materialize, and he might go in and order breakfast.

Finally he stood on a corner of a busy street and watched a tall, skinny, black man panhandling. He watched how the guy did it, how he went for nuns, people alone, a woman in a business suit looking preoccupied, but not hurried. He let the people walking in pairs or groups pass by.

Also, whenever he approached anybody, he hunched his shoulders, let his chin fall and his eyes become downcast. He shuffled his feet and mumbled softly. But when nobody was around, the guy stood up straight and didn't shuffle. He didn't look at the ground. Howie thought, this is a good act.

He got up close. The guy had a story. "I lost my wallet. Wife is pregnant. I don't have a job, and I need to buy the wife some food. I don't even have bus fare." Howie figured it was partly the look—chin down, voice low—and partly the story.

So Howie moved to a different territory, a few blocks over. Right away he saw some nuns.

"Nice day today," he said. He smiled, but he kept his chin down.

The nuns smiled under their wimples.

"It would be even nicer if I had one more dollar to get a bus ticket to Cincinnati. I could go and stay with my sister. She said I could come and stay with her." He kept his voice low, and he mumbled and shifted his weight from foot to foot. He got the dollar. He told his story again, and then again, until he had three more dollars. Then he went to look for a place to eat breakfast. He wondered if maybe they didn't serve it at The Blue Moon. He started out for there and passed the black guy going into a party store. The guy came out with a paper bag and sat down on the edge of the curb and drank from his bottle without taking it out of the bag. Howie sat down next to him.

"Mad Dog," the guy said.

"What?" Howie said.

"What's your name?" the guy said.

"Ace," Howie said.

"Ain't seen you around before," the guy said. He had a thick southern accent and mumbled into his bottle, so Howie could barely understand him.

Free meals seemed to be what this guy knew about. Salvation Army was the guy's best suggestion, but you had to listen to the "God lectures." There were a few other places like that. The shelter on Brush Street was another the guy thought was good.

Howie figured he didn't need this advice. He'd get his own food, and he wouldn't have to listen to anybody about anything, least of all God. He knew God as well as anybody. He could see Him in the sky, which was a creamy blue, the color of the rim on his mother's good china. He could see Him in the cement under his feet, cracked, and split, and dark with age. He knew God, and didn't need to be told about Him.

"Nobody never gets nothin' for nothin,'" the guy said. "I oughta know. Been on a chain gang. Been on a 'sembly line. Been everywhere. Tell ya where I wanna be right now. Here. Right here, man." He took a long swig of his Mogan David, then he got up and ambled off.

Howie went to find his breakfast, which he ate at Don's Coney Island—with the works, chili and onions—and then he did what he'd been wanting to do all his life. He went to the Detroit Public Library to read. What he wanted to do was spend the whole day there. So he found a small room which had tall leaded-glass windows that gave him a bright view of blue sky, grey buildings, and leafy treetops. He found a comfortable chair like the brown, naugahyde club chair in his mother's den, and he settled in to read. He chose *Our Oriental Heritage*, the first volume of Will Durant's, *The Story of Civilization*. It happened to be displayed on the shelf closest to the comfortable chair, and he decided that he would sit there in that room in that chair and put his feet up on the magazine table every day and read the whole series from beginning to end. It was something he'd always had in mind to do, and now it didn't matter how long it took. There was nobody to complain.

Howie could never understand why his father called him a bum when he was reading. What did it matter if the bed wasn't made? So what if there were a few dirty socks and maybe a baseball bat on the floor? It was his room. Couldn't he keep it any way he wanted? And what did it matter if the book was assigned by a teacher? Who cared? Couldn't he just read what he felt like reading? History, when he felt like history, and philosophy, when he felt like philosophy? What if he felt like biography, or fiction, or poetry, or geography, or psychology, or religion? Could any of this be bad? He thought about it for a while and decided his father was crazy. There was nothing to do about it—that was that—and he settled into his reading, which he did happily for some time, until he had gotten as far as Sumeria. Then he looked up and saw the big, beefy guy, the one from the men's john. The guy sat down at a table and opened a book.

"Hey," Howie said, softly.

The guy didn't look up. Howie could see the title of his book, *NAPOLEON BONAPARTE, An Intimate Biography*.

"Hey," Howie said again. The guy finally looked up, but it took him a minute to focus on Howie.

"Thanks, Man. You saved my life last night."

"What?"

"Thanks. I appreciated what you did."

The guy shook his head. "I didn't do anything."

"Well, thanks for nothing."

The guy nodded.

"Name's Ace," Howie said.

"Duke," the guy said.

"You like reading?" Howie asked.

Duke nodded. "History," he said. He had ash-colored hair that Howie thought must have once been white-blond. It was grown past his ears and had a spikey look, as if he'd just gotten out of bed. "The history of the whole world," he said, pushing his hair off his forehead.

Howie nodded.

"France, Italy, Poland, Egypt. Greece. Africa. South America... knowing... that is all I have left to do. I can't do anything else," Duke said.

Howie leaned forward in his chair.

"There isn't anything I don't want to know. Look at this book." He held the book up. "This book tells you everything you need to know about Napoleon. I mean, well . . . ." He looked down at the open page. "For example. Here's something interesting! How and why Napoleon was able to take the Italian Alps when France had been unsuccessful for three years in winning anything there."

Howie folded his arms and rested his elbows on his knees.

"Let's start with the army. Well, first I have to tell you what it was before the revolution. A big joke. A parlor game. These guys were dancing the minuet. Rules were everything. It was just ridiculous. Listen. Two armies would meet, and slowly deploy into long, perfectly dressed lines. Can you picture it? There they were—whole armies—in parallel columns, each column equidistant from each other, in perfect alignment, in perfect step. Okay, so then they'd go at it. Bang. Bang. They might as well have had pop guns. After a while, no more than a few hours, sometimes less, each army, or I should say team, withdrew to its camp. There was hardly a drop of blood. Battles were almost always a draw. War just went on and on, indecisively. Nothing happened. Boar hunting was more exciting."

Howie nodded.

"But then," Duke continued, "came the revolution. France now knew it was a nation. Look, this had happened before. In Elizabethan England and Philip II's Spain. A country gets an idea of itself. Wow. Bango. Anything can happen. The lines break up. Passion. Blood. Things change. People move up and down. It's exciting. And let me tell you, when there are stakes... oh, sure people get hurt, people die, but people also do *anything to win the game*. That's it. Win the game. Now here we are in France. NCOs rise up to be generals, and troops are trained in a hurry. They can't fool around with perfect lines, tidy maneuvers, dance steps. These guys hit and run. They'll do anything, and they'll do it fast. There's no textbook anymore. These guys are loose. A single column? Or, like Carteauz, a 'column of three'? Are you kidding? And let me tell you these guys had been terrific on flat land. They had been hooting and howling and taking every battle. But could they do it on that treacherous up-and-down country of the Italian frontier? We're talking tough terrain here. France had been losing badly on that ground. It was a rough game. It was a game of…well, as Napoleon put it…'We have been playing for three years in the Alps and Apennines a perpetual game of prisoner's base.' He wanted to end that game. And you know why he could do it?"

Howie shook his head. "Have you memorized that whole book?"

Duke nodded. When he nodded, he seemed to use his whole body, even his shoulders moved forward and back. "More or less," he said. "It's nothing I try to do. It just happens."

"You mean you remember everything you read?"

"Yes." Duke said. "But let me go on. Napoleon had four qualities that made it possible for him to do what he had to do in the Alps. Now this is interesting…to start with, he possessed a particular kind of physique characterized by a broad chest and big lungs. The big lungs inhaled deep chestfuls of air."

Duke inhaled deeply several times, closing his eyes as he did. "To oxygenate his blood," Duke said. He took several short breaths, and then another two or three big ones. "And this generous supply of oxygen provided him with an unusually quick rate of metabolism. 'Marry us quickly', is what he said to the registrar the day he married Josephine. Josephine's real name, by the way, was not actually Josephine, but Rose, which he didn't like, so he called her Josephine. But back to my point, which is that this was one example, from hundreds, of a pulsating activity which made Napoleon not only desirous of, but capable of, doing things really fast. Utmost speed." Duke snapped his fingers. "Speed," he said and took another full breath.

"Secondly, Napoleon was able to get along for a few days at a time on very little sleep. The guy could go on and on and on. He'd just ride all night. He'd make up for those long nights in the saddle by snatching a half-an-hour of sleep here and there, whenever he could. You might think this wouldn't work, but I've done some studies, and it has been proven that the first hour of unconsciousness rests the body fully as much as three hours in the middle of a full night's sleep. You don't believe that, but it's true. And that is how Napoleon, with quick naps was able to keep up his incredibly tremendous activity for eighteen and twenty-hour days."

Howie didn't say anything. Duke kept on talking for more than an hour. He completed the list of attributes which enabled Napoleon to do what no Frenchman had been able to do in the treacherous Alps—his eye for topography, his abilities as a gunner. He recited a stunning account of Napoleon's entire Italian campaign. It was filled with minute details, small asides, personal stories, things that some historians had said and that others had refuted.

Howie was enthralled. He was sure Duke knew more than any of his history professors had ever known—and that was a lot of professors from three different universities—and on that first day, by the time the blue sky, framed in the tall leaded-glass window, had turned to pink, the two were good friends, and they put away their books and left together. They walked down the long, marble stairway, laughing and talking.

"But why," Howie asked him. "Why Napoleon? What did he have, I mean besides big lungs and genius?"

Duke put his hands in his pockets. He stood at the foot of the stairs and looked at the wall behind Howie.

"Decision," Duke finally said. "He had decided his game. And he had decided to win it. It's as simple as that."

73

Howie decided then and there that Duke was the friend he'd always wanted. He thought he could sit and talk with Duke forever about everything in the world.

But, suddenly, as they were about to pass through the door, Duke seemed to change. His eyes glazed over, narrowed. The space between his brows furrowed. His mouth began to open, then shut, as if he was talking, but he wasn't. Then he started shouting. "WHAT'S CHU STARRIN' AT?" He opened his arms and stepped toward a young couple. Both were thin and pale and had many books under their arms.

He advanced toward them, putting his face close to their faces, and waving his arms menacingly. "WHO DO YOU THINK YOU ARE?"

A tall man wearing a red jacket appeared quietly beside Duke. "Duke," he said softly. He did not look at Duke's face but kept his eyes on the two young students, whose own eyes were wide and frightened. Their mouths were hanging open. "It's time to calm down now," the man said. He kept his voice low and even.

"YOU'RE A COUPLE OF SLIMY GREASEBALLS," Duke shouted at the students. He stepped closer, putting his face in front of the students' faces, putting his nose close enough to touch the nose of the boy.

"Now, Duke, you know you're just about to go. You're going to leave these two kids alone, and you're going to walk out the door . . . ." The man still didn't look at Duke's face or raise his voice.

"THEY WERE STARIN' AT ME," Duke shouted. He was still excited, but he had stopped waving his arms, and he was no longer moving toward the students.

"They didn't mean to stare. They're sorry they did." His arms were at his sides, and he did not raise his voice.

Duke was wild-eyed, but he took another step away from the students.

"That's good, Duke. You know these kids are really sorry they stared at you. They're going to leave now."

The students, their faces white, their eyes opened wider, even, than before, looked to the man, who motioned with his chin that they leave. They backed away toward the check-out counter.

"See Duke, the kids are going, and now you can go, too," the man said.

Without saying another word, Duke walked out the door.

Howie followed him and heard him talking to himself under his breath, but he could not make out what he was saying. He followed for about a block and a half, maybe two, until Duke stopped mumbling, and Howie called out, "Hey." But Duke didn't turn around. "Hey, Duke," Howie shouted and began to jog until he caught up. It wasn't so easy, since Duke was longer limbed and moved faster. Finally Duke turned to look at Howie, and Howie could see he was still wild-eyed and didn't know him.

Howie found a spot on the street to do his begging. He got enough for dinner, but not enough for the place with no name, or for any place with rooms and beds.

He didn't know where he was going to sleep, but then he saw Mad Dog sitting on the curb. He sat down next to him and asked him about a place. He figured even if he had to listen to the God lectures, he'd do it. Just for this one night. Anybody could do anything for one night.

"You gotta be thinkin' all day, where you gunna be sleepin'," Mad Dog told him. "You gotta know before it's dark."

"Well, I don't." Howie said.

So Mad Dog told him where to flop. "Don't tell nobody," Mad Dog said. "Do ya hear? Nobody. When people starts ta know, starts gettin' crowded, then somethin' happens."

"Okay," Howie said.

"I mean it. Don't spread it aroun'."

So Howie went to an abandoned warehouse in Greek Town. It was a large, red brick building, four stories high. He found an unlocked back door and walked in. The place was empty except for an old woman. She had a round face and odd hair that looked like steel wool that had been combed down flat. She wore several layers of ragged clothing that seemed to be the same color as her hair. Later Howie saw there was a man, too. He had a long white beard, was thin as a stick, and moved like a marionette. The woman's name was Lusa, and the man was called Humph, or something that sounded to Howie like Humph. Neither said much to him. Each stayed in a different corner of the warehouse and made a private place by piling up screens and boxes and tables that had been left about.

Howie liked everything there. He liked the wood floors that were covered with sawdust, and he liked the way it all smelled of cedar. So he set out to make his own private nest. He found some metal shelves, and a wooden table, and some old curtains and dragged everything to a niche in a corner between two posts. He pushed some extra sawdust around on the floor of his spot and used some shredded packing material he found in a box to make a bed under the table. What more could he ask for? He decided to live there forever. He could tell his sister-in-Cincinatti story on the street for meal money, eat breakfast at Don's Coney Island or The Blue Moon, read *The Story of Civilization* in the back room at the library all the day, and then flop at the warehouse.

It was a perfect life, for about two weeks. He had read as far as *The Mind and Art of Old Japan* and was as happy as he ever expected to be. Even the weather was glorious with mild, sunny days and cool, breezy nights. It was a picture-book autumn. Howie had never liked autumn. It always came at the same time that school started, and he was always angry and unhappy when he had to sit at a desk in a classroom. But now he walked with a light, loose-limbed step and he smiled a lot, forgetting about his anger. Howie also forgot that winter was coming.

Each day, he met Duke in the library. They talked and read together. Sometimes Duke would get kicked out for getting in people's faces; then he'd go back to the place where he slept—in a box outside Detroit General Hospital behind the heaters. Howie didn't like to go there—something about the box that Duke slept in. But there was a shower at the hospital, and Duke showed him how to go in there after five o'clock and use it. Every few days he would take a shower and then go alone for a burger or a hot dog. Then he'd go to his spot under the table at the warehouse for the night. That's how he liked it. Separate. Private. Trouble was, each night there would be another new person or two at the warehouse. Slowly, it was filling up.

One of the new floppers was mean. He riled everybody up, but Howie tried not to have anything to do with him; he stayed in his own spot and hated the noise whenever it started. Everything blew up one night, when the guy took over Humph's spot. First he moved his own collection of things from a storage closet—a winter coat, a coffee pot, a salami and a loaf of bread—and he lined them up on Humph's table. Then he threw Humph's things into a pile in the middle of the floor. When Humph came to sleep in his spot, the guy told him, "Fuck off." There was no reason for it, as far as Howie could see. The guy had his own spot, and there was still plenty of room for him to find a new one, if he wanted. Nobody did anything about it until the stranger took a punch at Humph. Humph collapsed like a rag doll on the floor. Then a bunch of them lifted the new man up from under the arms and carried him kicking and screaming to his own spot by the storage closet. "We like it quiet here," one of them told him.

"We'll carry you out the door, next time," another said.

But only a few nights after that, when Howie returned to the warehouse for the night, he found the broken windows repaired, the back door locked, and a night watchman standing in a brightly lighted window on the second floor, showing off his huge bulk and his huge billy club.

"Now what?" Howie said to Lusa. They stood on the sidewalk looking up at the hulking, dark shadow of the night watchman. The night watchman reminded Howie of his father. He had the same broad shoulders and the same flat shaped hat.

"We go to a new place," she said, shrugging, and she took him about two miles north to an old factory. She'd heard they had about twenty people working there weekdays, but that nobody was around at night. It turned out she was right. They found only one other person—a black man in a red and blue flannel shirt that looked almost new. In fact, he looked like a person who took showers every day. He didn't say much, but then, neither did Lusa. Howie found himself a spot and settled in. He wasn't as comfortable here, but he was relieved to find it so quiet after the raucus brawling at the warehouse. Then after a week, people began to come. It didn't take long before there were more than thirty sleeping among the tool and die equipment. It was a big place and there was room for everybody, but then one night the police showed up and arrested every one of them for drunken loitering.

At first, Howie was surprised and furious. He was herded like a cow into a police van, and then treated like a piece of dead beef when they got to the jail. The police pushed at him, then grabbed him. He could feel a thumb, hard as steel, cutting into his back, as one of them shoved him into a cell along with all the others from the factory. One of the new guys, somebody who'd only been there one night, unzipped his fly and urinated on the floor. He whistled while he zipped up, then he walked over to a corner to lean against the wall and fell asleep with his hands in his pockets.

Howie was standing so his shoes were next to the puddle. In the over-heated close quarters of the cell, the smell of urine, mingled with the smell of sweat, burned Howie's nostrils and the back of his throat. He went over to squeeze himself a place on the bench next to Humph. Humph turned to look at Howie. He leaned closer to Howie and patted his arm. His breath reeked of garlic and wine, and made Howie feel like throwing up. These people were a lot easier to like when they were far apart. And that is exactly how they all wanted to be. Far apart. That is what Howie wanted, anyway. He wanted to be far away and by himself. So he closed his eyes, and tried to think about the *Story of Civilization*. How could it happen that, in the whole history of the whole world, it had come to be that a person who didn't want to hurt anybody, who didn't want to steal from anybody, who didn't want to do anything but be alone, should find himself in jail?

"Lusa," Howie said. "You ever been in jail before?"

"Sure. Lotsa times," she said. "No big deal."

"I don't understand it," Howie said. "Why can't those guys who own that factory let us sleep there? It's not being used for anything else at night."

Lusa shook her head and shrugged.

"Well, it's just stupid," Howie said. "Just stupid. We're here in this hot, smelly cell. We're jammed in here, and the taxpayers are paying for it. We could be in that big, airy factory for free."

Humph laughed heartily and, as he did, he breathed his garlic breath in Howie's face.

"It's because of greed," Howie said. "Greed."

Lusa leaned her head against the wall and closed her eyes.

"It wasn't always like this. The Samoans weren't. And the Hottentots, the Chittagong Hill tribes of India, the Borneans, The South Sea Islanders . . . all of them shared their homes, their food . . . ."

Humph laughed again, but his laughter became a coughing spell.

"The land is like water and wind—that can't be sold." Howie said. "I forget who said that. Some Indians . . . somewhere . . . Omaha . . . the Omaha Indians."

Humph stopped coughing. He reached in and pulled a deck of cards from an inside pocket of his jacket. He shuffled the deck on his knee several times, then he held the deck in front of Howie's face and raised an eyebrow.

Howie shook his head.

"Sure?" Humph asked.

Howie shook his head again. "I don't play cards."

Then Humph had a taker from the other side of the cell, a young man who'd been at the factory for a short time, called himself Rollo.

Howie watched Rollo and Humph play pinochle for a while.

"YOU NEVER BEEN IN JAIL BEFORE!" Lusa suddenly shouted, pointing a finger at Howie.

"Yes, I have," Howie said. "Lots of times. Lots of times. In Cincinnati. Their jail is a lot cleaner than this one. Bigger, too."

"Must be the best jail ever built," Lusa said.

"It is now," Howie said. "They've remodeled it. Put orange tiles in the bathrooms. Every cell has a private bathroom."

The following morning, when they let him out, Howie gulped air like a madman. To Howie, it was wonderful—even that polluted city air—compared to the stench in the cell—tasted clear and sweet. But it was also cold. Whatever happened to warm breezes? Sunshine? Where was the blue sky?

His bones were aching from the damp chill. All his muscles were sore and cramping. He hurt all over. His head was throbbing, and he could not breathe. "It must be sinus," he thought, "or the flu coming on."

He set out to beg for his breakfast, but it started to drizzle. Almost everyone looked down at the sidewalk as they hurried past, as if they could avoid getting wet by stepping in the right place. Whenever he said good morning to a passerby, the person would look up and frown.

"Got a dollar?" he'd say.

"Later. No time," the person would say.

It took him most of the morning to get his breakfast, and then he had to think about where he was going to sleep that night. He asked around, got word about places to flop—empty apartments, duplexes or abandoned old mansions. He had a couple of places in mind.

By the time he had that settled, he had to start begging for dinner. That took even more time than breakfast. The drizzle had stopped, but it had become very cold. Nobody wanted to take off a glove and root around in the bottom of a purse or pocket.

"Indian summer is over," he heard on the radio at The Blue Moon. Howie didn't believe it, but it turned out to be true. Day after day, it continued to be cold and dreary. The sky remained the color of skimmed milk, and twice there were snow flurries.

Then one morning the sun began to shine, and the sky was a clear, cool blue. Even in the cold, people stopped to reach into purses and pockets. They smiled and steam puffed from their mouths. It was a good day for Howie. He got ten dollars and used most of it to sleep at a place like The No Name, but the next day he was sorry, because it was blistery with frigid winds and sleet. No one stopped to offer money. He wished he had enough to buy himself some dinner. He went to the soup kitchen on Brush Street, listened to the God lectures, and then he found himself a box and flopped next to Duke behind the heaters at Detroit General. As much as Howie liked listening to Duke's stories about the history of the world, he didn't like living in a box. It made him feel trapped.

After that he spent more and more time on the street, trying to get money to pay for a place to stay at night, and that left less and less time for the library. He wanted to eat, and he wanted to stay out of a box.

There were a few more good days, days when the sun shone and the air had no sharp edge, but by November, Howie began to do what he saw the others do. He stopped to pick up a coat at the Salvation Army and a jacket at Goodwill. He began to layer, like they did. Sometimes the others, if they were cold, would just take a coat out of a car left in a parking lot, but Howie didn't want to do that. Begging was one thing, but stealing was another. He wasn't going to steal. That was one thing he just wasn't going to do.

As it got colder and winter set in, whatever clothes he had were never warm enough, especially in the early morning and late afternoon, so he began to watch the others. They'd carry paper bags with sweaters and jackets in them, and, as the weather changed, they'd put on more and more clothes and stuff rags and newspapers inside their sleeves.

Howie did what they did. He'd stash the bag full of rags and sweaters at the party store while he was working for his supper. The storeowners never minded. When he went back to collect his things, he'd sometimes buy himself a bottle of cheap wine. That was another way to keep warm. It didn't help much.

He was spending more and more time outside, just trying to get enough money for dinner. He'd think of ways to make it easier for people. He'd approach them while they were standing by the parking meter with a glove still off, a wallet still out. He'd take whatever they had ready, a nickel, a quarter. He'd stand by the entrance to a parking lot and catch women while they had their purses handy. Sometimes he got lucky, but not as lucky as he wished.

Howie missed his time at the library. He dreamed about sitting in his cozy chair and studying the development of civilization. He had finally finished *Our Oriental Heritage*, and begun *The Life of Greece*, but he had gotten only as far as *Crete*, which was chapter one. It was getting him down, and he thought of going home.

He thought of it a lot. He thought of his room, his comfortable bed, the brown naugahyde chair in the den, his mother's rose-colored living room with two white camel-back couches, her refrigerator always filled with fresh fruits and vegetables, and her cupboard shelves stacked with cans and boxes—rice and noodles, and cereals and soups. Once he even went so far as to stand at a bus stop, but when the bus came, and he was about to step inside, he thought of his father. "Here comes the bum. Didn't make it on your own, eh? Got a little too cold? Now you want to come back and lay around again. Eat our food. Throw your leftovers to rot on the floor."

Then he thought about his mother. "Now Seth, can't you just tell him you love him? Tell Howie you're glad he's safe." His mother opened her arms to him. "We love you, Howie. Don't you know we love you?" The smell of her perfume—roses, and something else, marigolds he often thought—was so strong, even the memory of it made him sick.

The first big storm of the season happened in late November. It closed the schools in three counties and tore down electrical lines. Phones were out. The shelter on Brush street was filled, and Howie was on his way to another shelter when he passed the social services office. He walked by, thinking, not me. Not me. That's one thing I'll never do. Never. Never. But when he reached the shelter and got in a long line, he thought, that is the only answer. Temporary, of course. He tried to get his two friends, Duke and Mad Dog, to do it, too.

"Come on, man," he said to Mad Dog. "You crazy to be standin' out here freezin' your ass off. Let's go get us some money."

"What chu gotta do da get that money?" Mad Dog said.

"Nothin,' just go to the agency. Apply," Howie said. "Easy."

"Nothin' easy in this world." Mad Dog said.

"This is," Howie said.

"Fur you, maybe." Mad Dog shook his head.

"Nothin's hard for you, man. A guy like you?" Howie said. He'd heard all the stories about Mad Dog. People told how he had broken from a chain gang down south and started running and kept on running until he got to Detroit, how he'd worked in the factories until the jobs ran out, and then he'd started living in the streets. Howie thought Mad Dog could do anything.

"You know where this place is that you gotta go to?" Mad Dog asked.

Howie nodded. "I'll take you there."

Mad Dog shook his head.

"Just come with me," Howie said. "And let me show you what to do. I'll fill out the forms. No problem."

Mad Dog turned around and started to leave.

"Wait," Howie shouted after him. "Look. It isn't far. You can walk. It's six blocks south of here. Yellow brick building. Blue panels over the windows." He ripped off a piece of a brown paper bag and wrote down the street. "Be there tomorrow morning. I'll show you what to do."

"I don't need nothin'," Mad Dog said. He crumpled the paper and threw it on the ground. "Nothin'," he said. Then he turned and walked away.

"Mad Dog can't read," Duke told him.

Howie nodded. "But I would fill out the forms. He wouldn't need to. I told him that."

Duke shook his head, but he agreed to go. As soon as they got to the building, they saw they had to stand in line. There were about a hundred people in front of them, and they were moving slowly. It would take maybe an hour, give or take, Howie thought, and he did not know how long Duke could last in a public place. He just hoped they could stay long enough to get the forms. He figured if they could do that, they could take the forms back to the heaters at Detroit General, and then he could finish the rest by himself.

"What did Napoleon do, in the end?" Howie asked. "While he was in exile on St. Helena?"

"I'm glad you asked," Duke said. "Napoleon was Napoleon. He remained himself. Unbroken in spirit," Duke said and followed as Howie pulled him into the line. "He liked to say his body might be held prisoner, but his soul was still free." Duke became so engrossed in telling the story of Napoleon's last five and a half years, he did not notice anybody around him, and they advanced to the glassed-in window.

The woman behind the glass handed them some papers. "Fill these out," she said. "In triplicate. Have your driver's license and your social security cards ready at the next station. Follow the yellow arrows."

"Come on, Duke," Howie said and grabbed his elbow.

" . . . And so Napoleon's body was laid on the billiard table. Antonmmarchi deftly opened the cavities of the thorax and stomach. What he observed was a very extended cancerous ulcer. Napoleon had died of cancer of the stomach . . . ."

"And then what happened?" Howie said. He pulled Duke along the path of the arrows to the end of another long line. Howie wasn't sure Duke would last much longer. He thought he would get him started on Winston Churchill—his newest obsession—as soon as Napoleon was buried, but then Duke hunched his shoulders, and began pacing back and forth in small circles.

"What's this?" he said. He squinted at the papers, holding them away from his body, then putting them close to his nose. "These words are too small. I can't see them."

"Just put your name here," Howie said and pointed to the spot.

Duke shook his head. "No sir," he said. "I don't sign anything I don't understand. That's one thing I know about public life. You don't sign anything you don't fully comprehend."

So Howie read the instructions, conditions, and warnings out loud. Duke didn't understand anything Howie said, so Howie read them again, and explained each item over and over.

"You don't want to know this, do you?" he finally said.

"This is all crap," Duke said.

"Don't you see, you've got to listen to this. It's important. It's just as important as Winston Churchill and Napoleon Bonaparte."

"WHATCHU STARIN' AT?" Duke yelled. He was going for a frazzle-haired woman who clutched a baby in one arm and hung onto the hand of a whimpering toddler with the other. He craned his neck, pointing his chin, getting ready to pounce.

Howie quickly hooked Duke's elbow with his own, and speaking gently and calmly, he shuttled him out the door. When they were outside, he walked silently beside Duke, waiting until he was back to normal again.

"Look," Howie finally said. "Give me your driver's license and social security card, and I'll get the stuff processed. No problem."

Duke shook his head. "Don't have any of that."

"What?"

"Don't have a driver's licence. Don't have a social security card."

"What?"

"DON'T HAVE ANY OF THAT STUFF," Duke yelled. He started to wave his arms and step toward Howie, backing him off the curb into the street.

"Okay, okay. I'm sorry," Howie said.

"DON'T BUG ME, MAN," Duke screamed.

The next day, when Howie went back to the agency, he stood in another long line. It seemed much longer than the one he'd stood in the day before, but he thought it might be because he was alone.

When he reached the glassed-in window, he handed his driver's license to a young woman who wore round wire-rimmed glasses that had slipped down her nose. They magnified her eyes, so it seemed they were as large as the lenses and bugged out as far. She looked at the license carefully, as if she could see more with her giant eyes than others did with their normal eyes.

"What do *you* want money for?" she asked, peering at him. Her eyes were the size of silver dollars and the color of cold-blue marbles.

"To eat," he said.

"With this fancy address, you need food money?"

"I don't live there anymore."

"But your family does," she said. "They could help you." She narrowed her eyes, and they became guarded and wise as a cat's.

"My family has had a reversal of fortune," he said.

"You'll have to show proof of that," she said. "Hope you can get somebody to believe it."

So Howie decided to change his address. He asked around and found a man who made fake I.D.s and had him make one with an address around the corner from The No Name.

When he went back again to the agency, he was careful not to return to the woman who had big eyes again. When he saw the line he was in was headed for her, he moved to another.

Finally, he ended up in a room filled with desks. He sat facing a dark-haired woman whose long bangs fell over her eyes and almost entirely hid them. He thought she looked like a young deer hiding in the brush and was not nervous, while she asked him questions about his last employment, his last school enrollment, his next of kin. He told her how he'd moved from Cincinnati after his father had died.

She wrote down everything he said. "We'll call you in about a month," she said.

"I don't have a phone," he said.

"Come back then."

"Can you make it sooner?" he asked.

She shook her head. "It might be longer."

"Will I get the money then?"

"Maybe," she said.

"I really need that money," he said.

"You'll probably get it," she said. "If everything checks out okay." She placed his file on top of a pile of folders on her desk; then she glanced at her watch.

So he went to the shelter on Brush Street and offered to sweep floors and wash dishes, even though he knew he would have to listen to the God lectures. Lectures had always been his downfall, especially teacher lectures.

There was a teacher at the shelter, a woman whose name

was Bea. She had received the word from God to leave her job as a first grade teacher and to manage this shelter, where there were souls who needed her more than her first graders.

Howie didn't like her, but he was doing his best. He'd been there five days when Bea decided to help him.

"Howie," she said. "You're so smart. So smart." It was nothing new to him, and nothing she hadn't said before. "It's just a crying shame to see you here," she said. "Like this . . . ." She raised her arm, as if to raise his status. "Howie. The time is drawing near. You must make a decision to *put God first*. You put God first and then everything falls into place. You'll see, God is the Heading. Everything else fits under that. Believe me. Your life will be in order. It will make you happy."

Howie kept on sweeping and didn't say anything. He knew how to handle Bea.

"Howie," she said. "Howie. Save yourself. Just let God into your heart. Let him take your troubles as His own. Just ask Him. Ask Jesus, God's only son, who died for all of us, who is there for only one reason—to help us with our daily troubles—just ask Jesus to help."

Howie stopped sweeping. "Jesus," he said. "What should I do?" He stood there for a few seconds; then he hung up his apron and turned to go.

"What are you doing?" she cried.

"Jesus told me to go," he said and he walked out the door. When he got outside, he didn't know what to do. "Jesus," he said, whistling, "It's so cold."

He looked around. He saw a Buick Electra parked a few feet away. He peered inside to see if there was anything he could borrow—a coat, a pair of gloves. Nothing. Just a pile of newspapers on the back seat.

Mad Dog came by and caught him looking in. "I'm gunna show you somethin,'" he said. "It's time."

"Naw," Howie said. "There's nothin' here."

Mad Dog nodded. He reached into the pocket of one of his jackets and pulled out a wire hanger. "See, man, ya gotta do this fast. Ya gotta spend no time on gettin' in." While he talked, he slipped the wire through a crack between the window and the frame, unlocked the door, opened it and slid onto the front seat.

"Somebody's gunna see us," Howie said.

"So. Who you think's gunna turn you in? What you think they's gunna say?"

Howie stepped from foot to foot. He was shivering.

"Now look it here. First thing you need is this here." Mad Dog pulled a crowbar from another pocket.

"Ya take this and you just rip out all this pretty stuff here. See?" Mad Dog began to rip the front panel from the car.

"You're leavin' this guy's car a mess," Howie said.

"He'll get it fixed," Mad Dog said. "Rich guy like this. He got the money."

"What if a cop came by right now?"

"No problem." Mad Dog stopped to look at Howie. "You cold?"

Howie nodded.

"You hungry?" Mad Dog asked.

Howie nodded.

"Get yur' ass in here. This guy, owns this car. He ain't cold. He ain't hungry."

Howie spit on the ground.

"You gunna learn a thing or two? Or you wanna be dumb?"

Howie got in the car and bent down low next to Mad Dog.

"Now look it here. You can freeze yur' butt till next May, or you can get smart. What's it gunna be?"

Howie didn't move out of the car.

"You gotta do somethin'. Ya can't learn nothin' from watchin'. Here. Pull."

Howie hesitated a second, then he pulled, and the front panel came completely off.

"Now, here. See these knobs? Pull these off."

"With what?"

"Hands. Dummy. Just pull."

Howie pulled the knobs.

"Now. See those nuts there behind each knob? Ya gotta use this on 'em." Mad Dog handed Howie another tool. "Just take em' off. Like this."

Howie took the nuts off.

"Okay. Here. See these?" Mad Dog pulled another tool from another pocket. "Wire cutters. Just cut the wires and that's it."

Howie cut the wires.

"Now ya reach in unner here, and yank it. Like this. See?" Mad Dog gave a yank. "You pull it," he said.

Howie pulled.

"Congratulations," Mad Dog said. "Now take this to Harol's over on Lawrence street. You know where it's at. He'll pay you good."

"What if I see a cop on the way?"

"Don't. Don't see no cop."

Howie was turning onto Lawrence Street when he saw a big guy, dressed in black, swaggering toward him. The guy stood in front of him, blocking him. He put his hands in his pockets. Howie looked down at the guy's boots. They were fancy—western style—with purple and red tooling, and he wore a leather jacket. He was a dude all right. Howie looked up at the guy's face. It was long and narrow. He had dark eyes. I know this guy, Howie thought, but he didn't know from where. Then he remembered. Moe. The guy from the game. The guy from the men's room. The Doberman pinscher.

"Moe?" Howie said.

Moe stood real close to him, looking down at him. "You been lookin for me?" Moe said.

"Yeah. I owe you something. I've been trying to get the money together."

"You got it together yet?"

Howie nodded. "What do you think about a car radio, and five bucks?"

Howie felt the blow, like a hammer, pounding his jaw. He fell to the ground and wasn't conscious when Moe took the radio, five dollars he had in his back pocket, two of the jackets he was wearing and a scarf he had around his neck.

When he came to, Howie put his hand to his face. He touched his nose, his cheek, his mouth. His lips were numb and his face burned. He felt an empty place where his front tooth had been. When he took his hand away, there was blood on it. There was blood on his shirt sleeve. His body hurt all over. He pulled himself up, and walked unsteadily to Detroit General.

A police car slowed as it passed him. He didn't look at the cop. The car speeded up again and drove away.

Guy doesn't give a shit if I've been beat up, Howie thought.

When he got to Detroit General, he went into a bathroom and looked at himself in a mirror. His face was swollen; his mouth was puffy and hanging open with a dark gap where his tooth had been; his eyes were wide and round and bulging. There was blood in his beard, on his shirt, dirt in his hair, on his pants. *I can't go anywhere. I can't get on a bus and go home, if I wanted to. I'm a grounded fish.* He was shaking, and he thought it was from the cold. It came to him that he might never get warm again. He wasn't sure if he could stand it.

Until this moment, the hardships, the cold, the hunger had all been part of the trip, the way cold is part of skiing. But now that he could not simply take a shower, put on a clean shirt and leave, he was no longer a tourist. This was no longer a trip.

The gap in his mouth was his mark, the badge of a native. He knew if his mother saw him, she would cry. His old school buddies would laugh in their beers. An employer would not hire him for a job. He was really a bum. Duke, Uncle Sam, Mad Dog—he was one of them. He was a person with something missing.

Howie was buying some pot from Rollo at the moment his father's Lincoln Town Car drove by. When he spied the car, Howie stashed the nickel bag in his jacket pocket and tied his scarf over his mouth. Then he tried to get lost, backing into the shadow of a recessed door, but his father didn't give up. He parked the car and started walking. Then he stood on the corner and whistled, as if he wasn't looking for anybody. Howie watching him carefully, stayed where he was, but his father went straight for the doorway.

"Hi," he said, when he came to the edge of the shadow of the door.

"Hi," Howie said, still standing in the shadow.

"Just came down here to see if you needed anything," his father said.

"No." Howie said. He couldn't afford to say much; he didn't want his scarf to slip. "Don't need a thing."

"You feeling okay?" his father asked.

"Who told you I was here?"

"Nobody. I just figured."

"I'm feeling fine. Everything's great. I'm really happy."

"Well, here's something, even if you don't need it." His father held out some bills.

It looked like fifty dollars—two twenties and a ten—to Howie.

"Take it," his father said. "No strings."

Howie was tired. He didn't feel he had enough energy to beg for food. He had been spending more and more time in the library reading and listening to Duke talk about history. He'd stolen a couple of radios and smoked some pot. At night, he'd flopped wherever he could find a place, sometimes a shelter, but most often, he'd get a box and move in next to Duke. He couldn't find a box that he liked. They were all too small. When he rolled over, he hit the edges. There was just no way to get comfortable. He could never sleep. He thought he might go as crazy as Duke. He thought maybe it was lack of sleep that gave Duke his fits.

The day before, when he'd bought the marijuana, he didn't smoke it. He sold it for a profit and then slept at The No Name. He figured if he didn't need a bed, he wouldn't need to sell pot. But then he figured selling pot was easier than stealing a radio. And it didn't make a mess of anybody's car. He figured he'd get through until spring. Then he'd pull himself out of the box for good.

"Go ahead. I don't care what you buy with it," his father said.

Howie took it. He thought it would give him a bed for a few nights. If he didn't need a bed so bad, he'd never go this low. This was the lowest he could go. It made him feel short of breath and dizzy, the way being in a box made him feel.

The next day, he went with Duke to warm up at the library. He wasn't looking for a book, he didn't even want to read; he just wanted to find a place to sleep in the stacks. He couldn't get enough sleep. He walked up and down the aisles looking for a spot to lie down and stretch out, when he came across a book about poker. *Oswald Jacoby on Poker*. Poker was as far from his mind as his tooth was from his mouth, but the book was on the floor, so he picked it up. He read the first page.

"There is a popular misconception that, since poker is a gambling game, it is a game of pure luck. Actually, nothing could be further from the fact. Poker is the one game where a player may hold bad cards all evening and still come out a winner."

Howie could not imagine himself ever winning anything ever again—anywhere. He was a loser. He'd always been a loser. His father was right. His teachers, his aunts and uncles, everyone was right about him. He was too dumb, too lazy, too smart, too wrong . . . .

He stretched out on the floor, but he could not get comfortable enough to sleep, so he read the book.

"Poker is a game where there is a right technical play in every situation, and the winning player should know this correct technical play. But the winning player must go further. He must deliberately make the wrong technical play on a sufficient number of occasions so that the other players in the game will never be certain as to what he is doing."

Howie thought, "This is crap," but he kept on reading. He finished the book, found another one, and in several days he had read several books about poker. *Play Poker To Win*, by "Amarillo Slim" Preston, *Poker Strategy, Winning With Game Theory*, by Nesmith C. Ankeny, *The Complete Guide to Winning Poker*, by Albert H. Morehead, *Total Poker*, by David Spanier....

Howie was sitting on a bench down by the riverfront, reading one of his poker books. It was a mild day, clear and dry. The sun was shining for the first time in days and gave to everything—the sidewalks, the buildings, the people passing by, the words on his page—a definite clarity, a crisp blueness. He looked up from his book and saw a beautiful blond in a white jacket coming toward him. As she came closer, he saw it was his cousin, Marilyn. She was with a huge guy, and they had a huge, black dog on a leash. Marilyn led the way. The guy followed with the dog.

Howie pulled his scarf over his mouth and slouched onto the bench hunching down, so his chin was touching in his chest.

"Hi couz," Marilyn called. She had her hair in a pony tail, and it swung from side to side as she walked. She had a great walk. It was energetic and bouncy. Howie had never seen Marilyn when she wasn't bouncy. He liked that about her, and he liked it that she was a person who took things up. Ballet dancing. Painting. Horseback riding. Whatever took her fancy. But he didn't want to see her.

"Hi," he said and coughed, holding his hand over his mouth. "I've got something," he mumbled. "You shouldn't be near me. You might catch it."

"I'm not representing the family," she said. "They don't even know I came. They would be mad if they did."

He started to laugh. The scarf dropped. She saw the gap in his mouth.

"Oh my God," she wailed. "What would your mother say? My God, how did this happen? When? Who did it? Why don't you come home?"

She carried on until Howie finally told her, "Turn it off, Marilyn."

Marilyn stopped talking and looked at Howie.

"It's just a tooth," he said, though he had not come to feel any differently about it than he had the day he lost it.

"You're right. You can always buy another one," she said. "Remember my friend Amanda? She got her tooth knocked out when she rode her bicycle into a tree, and she just went to her dentist and he put in another one. You can't even tell."

Howie nodded, thinking about Amanda with her blue eyes and her blue angora sweaters. "Sure," he said. He kept his eyes down but tried to get a look at the guy Marilyn had with her. The guy was beefy like Duke. He had the same color hair, but it was thick and all of it seemed to be together, growing in the same direction.

"Listen," Marilyn said. "I want you to meet my friend, Jeff. He came down here with me, because I was afraid to come alone."

Howie nodded to Jeff.

"And this is Skipper, Jeff's dog. Isn't he gorgeous?" She patted Skipper on the head and rubbed his neck. "He's a Bouvier," she said. "They're fierce dogs. Very fierce. But Skipper is a sweetheart. Aren't you Skipper?" She put her face next to Skipper's nose and let him lick her. Then she puckered her lips and made as if she would kiss him. "Nice Skipper," she said. "Such a dear, dear, doggie." She made more noisy, wet, lip sounds and sweet talk. Skipper lifted his ears and barked, throatily.

"Nice to meet you, Skipper," Howie said. "Did you bring a gun, too?"

But Marilyn was looking around now, taking in the sights. "What else is new?" she said.

"Not much. Begging is hard work. It takes all day just to get dinner."

"What? You mean you beg?"

"Sure," Howie said. "It's what people do down here."

"You mean you go up to people and ask for money?"

"Yeah."

"You do?"

"Marilyn," Howie said.

"How do you do it? I mean what do you say?"

Howie shook his head.

"Look, if you don't like it, why don't you just leave?" Marilyn asked.

"Can't."

"For heaven's sake, why not?" Marilyn asked.

"Can't."

"Howie. You can do anything," Marilyn said.

"I don't have a tooth," Howie said.

"So go to a dentist."

"I can't."

"Silly boy," she said. She looked off in the direction of the river and stared for a while. Absently, she extended her leg and pointed her toe, a habit from the days when she was a ballet dancer. She didn't seem to be aware of it. "I have an idea," she said. "The family doesn't know about this. It's my own."

Howie usually liked Marilyn's ideas, but he didn't want to hear this one.

"Jeff's brother is going to open a bookstore," she said. "It's really cool. We just came from there. I mean we just came from the building. They're re-doing it, putting in a snack bar. And you can sit there as long as you want and eat a muffin, or a fruit salad. They're going to have lots of neat things. Honey yogurt dressing. Chocolate things. You can just drink coffee or tea, and read books, and eat little things. It's so cool. You'd love it."

"Sounds real cute," Howie said.

"That's what you should do, couz. You should go to this bookstore and drink tea and read all day."

"Yeah," Howie said.

"You could just sit there and be warm. You could even work there. That would be real cool. You could just talk all day about books and drink coffee and eat donuts. You could wear real clothes like you used to wear. You could get yourself some cool boots, and nifty T-shirts that say *New Yorker* on them, or *Rolling Stone* or something."

"Yeah," Howie said.

"Well, couz. I guess I'm not going to move down here. If you need anything, anything, just give a call. Listen...." She reached into her purse and fished around on the bottom. "I don't have anything but this," she said. She held out a ten dollar bill. "Call me."

Howie took the money and watched Marilyn walk away with Jeff and Skipper. The dog's tail and the girl's tail were both swaying, but at different times and in different directions.

He pulled the poker book from his pocket. He opened the book and read: "On the fourth card, unless you hold a very high pair or have a four flush or an open-end straight, you should surely get out if anyone bets."

He shut the book. He was feeling low-down after he saw Marilyn. When he closed his eyes, he saw her hands. Her fingernails were polished. Soft pink. Not bubble gum pink. Now he remembered it. *Dusty pink*. Dusty pink was her favorite color, the only color she would wear in junior high. "Everything has to be dusty pink," her mother told his mother. "Now she's doing her bedroom in it. At least she isn't crazy for purple."

Even though he had the ten bucks, he went to the Salvation Army to get a free dinner and met up with Duke. He stood in line next to him, while they waited for beef stew.

"Duke," he said. "What if there was this character in a book you were reading?"

Duke nodded without looking at him.

"Let's say there was this person living in . . . say . . . 1936."

Duke nodded.

"And this person was definitely a poker kind of guy."

"Yeah . . . ," Duke said. The line was moving swiftly. They had reached the beef stew. Duke took his bowl.

"But this guy couldn't play poker," Howie said.

"Yeah," Duke said.

"This guy read all the books, and he knew all the tricks, but he just couldn't do them?"

Duke nodded.

"What do you think?"

"Why does this guy want to play poker anyway?"

"Because," Howie said.

"Then I think he should just do it."

But Howie's bones were cold and his hope was frozen. "Naw. There's something about this guy. He likes knowing the tricks, you know what I mean? Understanding them, but not necessarily doing them." Howie thought Duke would understand this. It was his problem in life, too, knowing so much and able to do so little. "I mean, he likes knowing how to steal a car radio. He just doesn't want to steal it."

Howie believed with one part of his brain that what he meant was that he had some high moral standard that he didn't want to compromise, but he knew, really, that he meant there was something wrong with him—some little gismo in the brain gone awry. Maybe it was just a tiny shunt out of kilter, but it made all the difference.

"I can't go home," he told Duke.

Duke wasn't listening. His eyes were glazing over. His forehead was furrowing.

"I'll never go home," Howie said. "Never," he slammed his fist on the table to get Duke's attention.

But Duke's whole body was taut. He was staring at a guy across the room. Howie had never seen the guy before.

"Whatchu starin' at?" Duke asked. The stranger had thinning dark hair and wore a navy blue pea coat. He didn't look big.

Howie sighed. "Come on Duke, let's go," he said.

"I asked you, WHATCHU STARIN' AT?" Duke shouted, leaning forward in his seat.

The guy shook his head. Duke got up and walked across the room, stepping on people's feet, knocking over a chair.

He stood close to the stranger. His knees were almost touching the man's chest. Duke bent down, put his face right up close, eye to eye, nose to nose, with the face of the stranger. The stranger pulled away. Duke moved forward.

Two men sitting near Howie jumped up and pulled Duke away and held him, while others grabbed the stranger and pinned his arms. It finally took six men to hold them apart.

"Come on, Duke. Let's go. Let's go for a walk," Howie said. He turned and started for the door.

Duke followed, still shouting, "FUCK THE BASTARDS, EVERYBODY LOOKIN' AT YA, SHIT-FACED FUCKERS, THEY THINK THEY KNOW SOMETHING. NOBODY KNOWS," he shouted to no one in particular. "NOBODY KNOWS."

Howie thought, so this is what I left home for...more shouting. Then it came to him that life gives you what it wants to give you. And for him, it was people shouting.

"NOBODY KNOWS," Duke yelled. "THOSE FUCKERS. THOSE FALSE-FACED FUCKERS."

Howie walked beside Duke for a while. "What if I did go home?" he finally said. "What if I just got on a bus and went home?" He thought Duke might answer him, but when he didn't, Howie thought about how things would be out there. Everything—his bed, his food, his clothes, his books—would all be charity. "He's not even good enough to be a bum," his father would say.

"I can't go home," Howie said.

Duke stopped. His face was calm, his eyes focused. He looked at Howie and blinked. "Why the hell not?" he asked.

Howie shrugged.

They started walking, headed for Detroit General.

"About this poker player," Duke said. "How bad does he want to play poker?"

"He wants to. But he can't," Howie said.

Duke nodded. His whole body—his shoulders and torso— moved when he nodded. "What year did you say this was? 1936?"

"Yeah," Howie said.

"Why can't he play?"

"Can't." Howie said. "He has some kind of poker phobia."

Duke nodded.

"You've played some poker yourself, haven't you?"

"Once. Maybe a couple of times," Howie said.

"You've been reading a lot of books lately," Duke said. "You want to play?"

"Naw. Who would I play with?"

"Me."

"You?"

Duke nodded. "I used to play poker," he said. "I was good. Had to quit when people started starin' at me."

"Too bad," Howie said. "If you still played, you could teach me."

"Oh, I could teach you all right," Duke said. "I could show you everything those books talk about. You know you can't learn poker from a book. Poker's the only thing you can't learn from a book."

They got themselves a deck of cards from the party store, and then they sat next to the heater behind the hospital, and Duke taught Howie everything he knew about poker. He told him the rules and the tricks of the games. Seven card stud. Five card stud. Draw. He told him when to open, when to sandbag, when to stay with a pair, when to raise, and when to stay after a raise. He told him to watch body movements and faces—glances, frowns, smiles—and he told him to be careful about bluffing, how to do it and how to guess if the other guy is doing it. He told him to watch everything all the time.

"Watch people when they glance to the left," he said. "It's just a little sideways peek, if you know what I mean . . . like this. See?" He slid his eyes quickly to the left without moving his head. "Look, if a player has a normal calling hand, he'll come into a game without a show. Nothing. No fuss. But a player with a good hand is going to consider raising. He might just glance, like this, see," He did it again. "He's going to want to see what the players behind him are doing. I mean on his left. To see if he can get some inkling as to what they're going to do. If he gets the feeling that two or three of them are going to call, he sandbags. If it looks as if they are all going to drop out, he raises. But, now listen. When you see this glance, see it, sneaky, like this?" He did it again. "No matter what the player does, even if all he does is call, you can be damn sure that his hand is strong enough for a raise. Got it?"

"Shit," Howie said. "How can I remember everything? It'll take me years."

"Naw. Just stick with me. We'll get you playing in no time."

"Forget it," Howie said. "It's stupid. I don't need to do this."

Duke shook his head. "Yes. You do," he said.

"Look, I screwed up once. I paid the price."

"It's like the horse thing. You know? Get back on the horse that threw you," Duke said.

"I don't care if I ever play poker. I never did," Howie said. "Who gives a shit?"

"Well, I give a shit. I want to do it. I want us to go in there, to Al's Place, and I want to play that poker game."

"You do?" Howie said.

"I want to keep my face still for one night. One night of poker. That's all I ask," Duke said.

Howie looked at him. He was thinking Duke could never do it.

"Quit looking at me like that," Duke said.

Howie didn't say anything, and Duke's eyes began to glaze. His mouth started opening and closing. He stepped toward Howie.

"KEEP YOUR FACE STILL," Howie shouted. "DON'T MOVE." Howie was sure that this wouldn't work, but Duke held himself still. He sat without moving until the fit passed.

"What you gotta be," Duke said, after he was himself again, "is a wooden Indian. That's how I want to be for two hours. That's all I want . . . And that's what you have to want, too. You have to be a statue."

"Like stone," Howie said.

"Yes. Like stone. You gotta make all your plays the same, identical way. So people can't read you. If you frown and complain to cover your good hand, people are going to know it." He shook his head sadly. "I really had it. I really had it."

"You'll have it again," Howie said, but he didn't believe it.

Duke shook his head. "Right now you're looking at me. Stop looking at me."

"I'm not."

"Well, DON'T DO IT ANY MORE," Duke shouted and moved close to him, but Howie didn't back away. Duke got his face in Howie's face and started to wave his arms and swear and carry on, but Howie didn't move, and then Duke calmed down. They practiced like that night after night, until Howie thought he had the game, and Duke thought he could be still long enough to play.

Then they set out for Al's place. The air was damp and cold, and the streets were full of puddles and edged with the grey crust of old snow. It was the kind of weather Howie always hated.

"As soon as I get enough money to buy a tooth, I'm going to move to Florida," he said. "The streets have to be better in Florida."

"Streets might be warmer, but they won't be better," Duke said.

Howie didn't trust Duke. Duke was a man who was not unhappy in a box. What could he know about the streets in Florida?

When they got to Al's Place, Howie stopped outside the door. "I don't want to do this," he said. "I don't want to get my face smashed in another time. I just don't."

"Don't worry about it," Duke said, and he pulled him through the door. Once they were inside, Howie knew he could not leave without a terrible scene with Duke. He wanted to turn and run, but he followed Duke to the backroom.

The guys were sitting at the table, Eagle, Red, Moe, Uncle Sam. Duke and Howie stood in the doorway.

"Sam, it's your friend. The wormy kid, and he's got his sidekick, Brute," Moe said.

Howie looked at Moe's boots—the purple ones with the red tooling. Howie's mouth felt dry. He licked his lips.

Uncle Sam looked up. "Hi Ace," he said. "Long time no see."

Howie pulled a ten dollar bill from his back pocket. He held it with both hands at arm's length in front of his nose. "I'm putting my money on the table," he said. "I want to play."

"Nope," Moe said. "No way."

"Here's the cash," Howie said. "I play 'til I lose. Then I leave. That's it."

"Nope," Moe said. He started shuffling the deck.

"Give the kid a chance," Uncle Sam said. "He's been around the block a couple of times, since he was here last."

Howie smiled, showing his missing front tooth.

Moe looked at Duke. Duke's eyes started to glaze over, and he stepped toward Moe.

Howie thought this is it. The end of my face. He grabbed Duke's arm. "Don't move," he said under his breath, but loud enough so that anybody could have heard.

Moe started to rise from his chair.

Red pushed his chair away from the table. The sound of its legs scraping on the floor was the only sound in the room. He stood, planting his fists on the table, his large shoulders hunched. He looked like a bull dog.

Duke didn't move, but he was wound up tight. The chords on his neck stood out.

"Get rid of your friend," Moe said. He was looking real hard at Duke, but Howie took a side step and was in front of Duke. He turned to face him and looked straight into Duke's eyes. "Two hours," he said. "Don't move for two hours."

"You can play if your friend leaves," Moe said. "That's it."

Howie shook his head. "He won't cause trouble."

"He does, and your face is mashed potatoes," Moe said. "I been looking for another chance at you. I really don't like your face."

Howie felt the way he did when he was sleeping in a box. He breathed deeply, but he couldn't get enough air. He sat down at the table, and Duke took a chair by the wall.

"The Brute's going to see our cards," Red said.

"You think they're in cahoots?" Eagle said.

"Naw," Moe said. "Not smart enough. But make him move anyway."

They all looked at Duke.

Duke moved his chair further away.

Red shook his head. "He's right across from Ace, lookin' at his eyes," he said.

So Duke moved further away.

Howie wanted to protest, but he knew better.

Finally, Red said, "Okay. Its okay. I just remembered the guy's got bad eyes. Let's start."

Moe glanced over at Duke, nodded, as if to say, well, okay, but then he kept glancing at Duke, turning his head to stare.

Howie saw Duke getting edgy, and he pointed a finger. "One night. That's all," Howie said. "One night."

Duke didn't move, so then Moe counted out ten dollars worth of chips for Howie, and they cut the deck to see who'd deal. Red pulled the high card, so he put five dollars in the pot. "The usual," he said, looking at Howie. "Five card Draw, guts to open." He dealt out the five cards.

"I check," Uncle Sam said.

"One dollar," Moe said.

Eagle threw his dollar on the table. So did Topper.

"I'll see you and raise a dollar," Howie said. He had a pair of aces, and he thought he had a good chance.

Then Sam took three cards, Moe took one, Eagle took three, Topper took three, and Howie took three. The draw gave him trip aces. So he was back. A winner. A winner. Then Moe bet another dollar. Everyone saw the bet.

It came to Howie. He looked to Duke. Duke was like stone. "I'll see your dollar and raise a dollar," Howie said.

"I'll see *your* dollar and raise you a dollar," Moe said.

Howie looked at Moe. Then Moe looked at Duke. All the guys looked at Duke.

Duke didn't move. He was a wooden Indian.

Howie called.

"Pot's right," Red said. "Who's got what?"

Sam laid out his cards; he had two pairs—jacks and tens. Moe had three queens. Eagle had a pair of kings. Topper had two pairs—sixes and eight's. Howie showed his aces. Then he had twelve dollars.

Topper shook his head. "I don't know," he said. "I gotta go."

"Me too," Eagle said. "I'm outta here."

"What? You guys can't leave," Red said.

"Stay," Uncle Sam said. "It's early."

Topper put on his jacket. "I'm busted," he said.

"Gotta catch a plane," Eagle said. He put his hat on.

"What about our game?" Red said.

"Let the big guy play," Eagle said.

"No way," Moe said.

"Let him in," Uncle Sam said. "He hasn't been any trouble, yet." So Duke got in the game. Howie kept looking at him thinking, *Be like stone. Be like stone.*

And Duke was. He played as if the history of the world depended on it. Two hours later, Duke hadn't thrown a fit, and Howie had eighty-eight dollars. He thought I'll quit at ninety-eight, but he looked at Duke and saw that his eyes were glazing over, narrowing. His lips were moving. "Time for us to go," he said.

"What's a matter? You turn into a pumpkin or something?" Moe asked.

"Yeah." Howie said.

"I'm not ready to leave," Duke said.

"Yes you are," Howie said and pushed away from the table.

Duke shook his head. His eyes were almost slits. He was leaning forward; his body looked taut. So Howie grabbed his arm and pulled him away.

"I'm cashing in," he said to Moe.

"No way," Moe said. "It's too early."

"Gotta go," Howie said.

Moe's eyes narrowed like Duke's, but he handed over the money. Stuck it in Howie's hand. Then Howie pulled Duke toward the door.

"But what about their game?" Duke asked.

"Plenty guys lined up for our seats," Howie said. "Come on, our Fairy Godmother is waiting." Howie kept pulling him until they were outside. Duke seemed to sober up when the icy, night-drizzle hit his face.

Then suddenly, two big guys in black leather jackets appeared. Their heels made fast, angry sounds, rat, tat tat, like stilettos, on the cement as they approached. They had their hands in their pockets, so it looked to Howie like they were holding onto knives.

"WHAT CHU LOOKIN' AT?" Duke shouted. The men kept on coming, but Duke looked at Howie, took a deep breath and started to calm down. "I'm not gonna do that anymore," Duke said. "I'm done with that. Cured."

Howie could see that one of the guys wore a hat like Eagle's. He had on Eagle's jacket. They got closer, he could see their faces. Eagle and Topper. Come back for their money.

"No, no, DO it," Howie shouted. "NOW'S THE TIME. GO FOR 'EM."

Duke shook his head. "I don't need to."

"YES, YOU DO. REALLY, GO FOR THEM," Howie said, "GO," and Duke did. He went for them both, screaming and waving his arms, moving at them like a bulldozer. He didn't care about knives. He didn't care about anything.

Howie started to pray. "God, forgive me," he said. "I'll never do this again. Any of it. I'll never beg. I'll never gamble.

I'll never use another person like I've used Duke. Never. Please, let us get out of here."

Duke kept on advancing, waving his arms and shouting, "WHO DO YOU THINK YOU ARE, YOU LOUSY, FUCKING, SCUM EATING PIGS...."

Howie thought, *What if they pull out their knives? What if they go for him? It will be my fault.* But the men turned and ran. Duke kept on shouting, until they were out of sight. He was like a machine.

Howie followed him until he was calmed down. It took several blocks. "I'm sorry," Howie finally said. "I ruined your cure."

Duke shook his head. "I would have gone off, anyway. Sooner or later."

Howie shrugged. "Maybe not."

"But I could have played an hour longer. You pulled me away too fast. You should have let me play longer."

Howie knew that wasn't true. "I'm sorry," he said. "How much you get?"

Duke looked at his feet. He shook his head. "Twenty-seven dollars."

"That's not bad," Howie said.

Duke smiled. "Maybe I'll have another chance," he said.

"Sure," Howie said.

They went to another saloon and drank a couple of beers. They talked about playing poker again some time, then Howie bedded down in a box near Duke's, behind Detroit General. He did not go to The No Name, because he was saving his money, but he could not sleep all night. I'll never live in a box again, he thought. Never. Never. I want to live like a person.

The next morning, he woke up as the sun was rising and caught a bus headed in the direction of his dentist's office. He walked in and put his name on the sign-up sheet, as if he had an appointment.

"How much for a new tooth?" he asked the receptionist. She was seated behind a glassed-in window. Howie had the feeling that he would always talk to young women who were behind glass.

"What?" she shouted. She stepped back as if he was coming toward her, as if there was no glass between them.

Howie couldn't remember her name, and he thought it was because she never remembered his. "Sarah. Sally. Your name's Sally right? Or is it Cindy?"

Her mouth dropped open. "Cindy," she said.

"I need a new tooth. How much will it cost me?"

"We'll have to ask Dr. Levin," she said. She went to find him.

Howie felt like gagging from the smell of the antiseptic, but Dr. Levin came right away.

He stepped into the waiting room and seemed unusually clean to Howie. He wore a bright, white coat, and his precisely cut, dark hair was combed smooth and was as shiny as enamel. His skin, too, seemed bright, and he smelled strongly of the antiseptic that was making Howie feel sick.

Dr. Levin looked him over. It took him a few seconds to smile. "Howie, Howie. We haven't seen you in such a long time," he said. His voice was loud and very jovial. Howie saw him looking over his shoulder at a woman who was sitting in one of the grey tweed chairs with a *Time Magazine* in her lap. He saw the woman raise her eyebrow at Dr. Levin. Dr. Levin didn't react.

"Sandy, squeeze Howie in right away, I'll take a look at his mouth."

"First you have to tell me how much and how long," Howie said. "I need a tooth." Howie smiled, broadly. "See?" he said.

"One hundred for a temporary partial. I can do it in a week," Dr. Levin said.

"Okay." Howie followed Sandy to an examination room. He sat down without a word and let Dr. Levin look in his mouth.

"Where ya been?" Dr. Levin asked

"Nowhere," Howie said.

"I saw your mother last week," Dr. Levin said.

Howie grunted. Dr. Levin was poking at his teeth with a metal pick.

"You have a shower lately, Howie?"

Howie grunted again.

"You need a shower, Howie, but I like your hair. That the new look? Long like that?"

Howie grunted.

"You look like Jesus. Here. You can rinse your mouth out now. Use that cup."

Howie swished the mouthwash around in his mouth. He'd forgotten what it tasted like.

"Now look. I can suit you up with a temporary, but the real thing will cost you about two hundred fifty, three hundred dollars, and there's some other work we'll have to do. You've got some decay here."

"Get me the temporary right away," Howie said.

"You know, if you don't start taking care of your teeth, you're going to lose every single one of them. You're going to have gum disease. You're going to have toothaches. You're going to have to have surgery...listen here, Howie, I love ya. I've known you ever since you were this high, but I'm not going to meet you here on a Sunday night for emergency treatment. You got that? Don't call me in the middle of the night for pain killers."

Howie reached into his pocket, drew out eighty dollars and put it on the tray next to the chair.

"I need a tooth," he said. "And a toothbrush."

"One week," Dr. Levin said. He handed him a blue toothbrush. "The brush is free."

Howie went back to live behind the heater with Duke, but now he knew he was a visitor, just passing through, not a resident. He liked sitting around by the heater, talking. He and Duke repeated the details of the poker game over and over, the way Duke always repeated the details of world history. Every day for a week, they went to the library. Duke read about Pearl Harbor, and Howie read "The Old Testament."

One day, he decided to check at the welfare office. He figured he wasn't going to get any money, but he thought, *Why not check it out?* He went to the head of the line to see if the girl with the giant eyes was behind the window. She wasn't.

So he stayed. He read an issue of *Time Magazine* he'd taken from Dr. Levin's office. He had read nearly the whole thing, when he got to the glassed-in window. There she was, Big Eyes.

"You again!" she said.

"You remember me?"

"I remember your address," she said.

He handed her his fake driver's license and his social security card. He smiled, showing her his gap.

"This isn't it," she said.

"What?"

"This isn't your address."

"It is now," he said. "The other one was old."

"Did your family move too?"

"Yeah. Like I told you before. A reversal of fortune."

"Yeah. Sure."

"Did my check come in?"

The woman looked through her files and pulled out an envelope.

"Here it is," she said.

Howie took it. He opened the envelope. "Yep," he said. "This is what I was hoping for."

"I don't get it," the girl said. Her eyes looked like blue marbles.

"Like I told you," Howie said. "A reversal of fortune. It happens."

The girl smiled, and he could see she had very small teeth.

"Here it is. One hundred fifty bucks," Howie said and handed the check to Duke. "You could do this. You could keep your face still for two hours once a month, and you could get this kind of money. Easy. A snap." He snapped his fingers.

The next day, Duke went to the welfare office with Howie. Before they got through the door, Duke thought somebody was staring at him. His eyes narrowed, and he started to move toward an old man with a cane. Howie pulled him away.

"Why, why can't you do it?" Howie asked him when they had walked for several blocks.

Duke shrugged. "I can't."

"You did it once."

"That's sometimes all you get," Duke said.

They lived for two days off the welfare money. They used up about thirty dollars. Howie counted out eighty more, enough for him to take a bus home, pay for his tooth, and have some left over. He gave the rest of the money to Duke, and he set off.

"You're on time," Dr. Levin greeted him. "This is a new habit?"

Howie didn't bother to answer.

Dr. Levin installed the partial in Howie's mouth and handed him a mirror. "Looks as good as ever," Dr. Levin said. "What do you think?"

Howie smiled. It was his old smile, the one he left home with, the one he'd had since grade school.

He began to notice the smell of mint. It smelled so good to him, he could hardly stop breathing long enough to say, "Looks good. Thank you."

As soon as he was out of the office, he found a pay phone at the end of the hall, and he called Marilyn.

"Whoa, cousin," she said when she saw him. "You need a shower. And some new clothes that don't . . . um . . . stink."

She took him to Jeff's house for the shower and into town for some new jeans, T-shirts, sweaters, a jacket, shoes and socks.

"I don't want anything fancy," he said when she pulled a red turtle neck from the shelf. He picked himself some plain things, the kind he'd always liked to wear, grey and blue, and brown. When he put them on, he felt the way he'd always felt when things were right.

"You look like somebody now," she said. "Like you used to . . . but you have to pull your hair back. It looks . . . um . . . you know . . . " She took the rubber band from her own hair. "This is how you do it," she said, and she made a ponytail for herself. Then she took it out again and gave the elastic to him.

"I know how to do it," he said. Then he did.

"Not bad," Marilyn said. "Come on. I'll show you the new bookstore. 'Course it's not quite done yet. But when you see it, you won't believe it was once a car dealership."

"I don't want to see it," he said.

"Silly boy," Marilyn said and drove there anyway.

Howie knew he would have to take a look. He was prepared to have even his low expectations disappointed, but the sight of the huge space, soaring ceilings, and many shelves filled with books gave his heart a rise. It was more than Marilyn had promised. There were comfortable-looking chairs and benches with pillows, many nooks and niches filled with sunlight, where a reader could burrow in. Spider plants and ivy, in glazed pots, were hung from high shelves. This was his kind of place, and Harold, Jeff's brother, was his kind of guy.

He had a rumpled look that Howie liked. He wore faded jeans and a striped shirt that looked as if it had never been pressed. He was growing a beard that didn't seem to be working out. Howie liked that, too. He was friendly but seemed to be thinking of something else while he talked. Another thing Howie liked.

"Howie's the one I told you about. The one who likes to read so much," Marilyn said.

Harold nodded, but his eyes were vague, as if he didn't remember.

Howie felt relieved to see Harold didn't care.

"The one who knows so much," Marilyn said.

"Marilyn," Howie said. "We've got to go now." He didn't like to rush into things, and he didn't like what she was doing—pushing him on Harold. How could she be so nervy?

"Well," Harold said. "It's been nice meeting you. I've got some unpacking to do here." He held out his hand, but he didn't look at Howie as he shook; he looked at a pile of books on the floor.

Howie looked at the books, too. *The Struggle for Europe, The Last 100 Days, Come as a Conquerer, The Gathering Storm, The Hinge of Fate, Closing the Ring, Their Finest Hour, Triumph and Tragedy....* Howie thought of Duke. Duke would love these books. He could talk about them for weeks.

"You need anybody to sell books here?" Howie asked.

"Have you had any experience?" Harold asked. He turned to look at him.

Howie didn't like the way he looked at him, judgmentally, like a teacher. He thought maybe this wouldn't work out. He shrugged and opened his palms to the ceiling, gave the guy a lopsided smile.

"What kind of books do you read?" Harold asked.

"All kinds. I read about history, psychology, philosophy. I read books about poker. I read Camus. Thomas Mann. Agatha Christie. I read the *New York Times* and *The Wall Street Journal*. The last book I read was the Bible."

"What?" Harold asked, as if he hadn't heard.

"I read anything," Howie said.

Harold looked him up and down. He rubbed the spot where his beard would be if it had flourished and stared off into space. Finally, he looked at Howie. "Five days a week, twelve to six, sound good to you?"

Howie found himself a place to stay. It was only one room in an old house that had been converted to apartments, but Howie liked the window. It had antique leaded-glass and gave him a view of a maple tree and a fenced-in yard, where a German shepherd spent a good deal of time. He didn't get a phone; there was no shower, but he could use the one downstairs. He refused to take most of the furniture his parents offered, but he did take a bed and a table, a set of shelves for his books, and a deck of cards, "for sentimental reasons only," he said. He never played another game of poker.

"I don't want to own a lot of things," he told Marilyn. "But I do want to know where I'm going to sleep, and I do want a female companion, if you know what I mean. I never found anybody down there."

His parents were thrilled. He had a job. They told all their friends. "Howie is turning into a real mensch." They began to leave college catalogs and law school brochures around the house whenever he visited them.

Howie never said a word to them about the catalogs or about his plans, but he told some of his friends and cousins, "It's a lot easier to work than to beg."

Twenty years later, Howie was still selling books, but not at the same bookstore. Harold went out of business, and Howie took a job at a newer bookstore down the street. He didn't like his boss at the new store, a man who lectured and told him what to do. He could never stand that, so he settled at a third place, where nobody gave him any rules, and people liked to joke around.

He still had all but that one of his own teeth, and he had a T-shirt that said "I know a little bit about everything." A good number of people must have believed the T-shirt, because he was the one they asked for at the bookstore whenever they had a question about a book.

Sometimes, people asked him about himself. He usually told them, "The streets taught me everything I know, but they aren't what they used to be."

He'd gone back few times. He'd found Duke at the library. They'd hung around for a while. Howie gave Duke some money, some clothes—jackets, gloves—and a few books. He'd found Mad Dog and given him some money, too. After a while, more and more time passed between visits, and then one day, he went back and Duke was gone. He looked in the library, behind the heaters at Detroit General, and at Al's Place.

Finally, he went to The Blue Moon for a burger and fries. He sat down at the counter beside a young girl, too young to be so tired looking. He could see she would have been beautiful; she had delicate features and blond hair, but her skin looked greasy; it was caked with make-up. Her face was swollen, and her eyes were glazed over, like Duke's had been when he was having a fit.

She leaned on her elbows and hunched her shoulders as she ate her fries, and her long hair touched the counter top. The tip of one strand landed in her ketchup.

"Ace!" Al shouted. "Haven't seen you around. Burger? Heavy on the onions? Extra fries?" Al's hair had gotten some grey in it, and he'd gained a pot belly.

"You remembered," Howie said.

Al smiled. "I remember everything."

"You seen Duke?" Howie asked.

"Not for a while. Uncle Sam's gone too. So's Mad Dog. Lots of new people coming in."

"Like this one. I never saw her before," Howie said, nodding toward the girl beside him.

"I been here," she said without turning her head.

"Name's Ace," Howie said. "I've been visiting my sister in Cincinnati."

"So that's why you haven't seen me." She turned to look at him. "You don't stay around here," she said.

"I used to."

She nodded. "I'm pregnant." She turned back to her fries.

"You on something?" Howie said.

"You selling?"

He shook his head.

"You want to buy?" she asked.

"Crack?"

"I know where you can get some," she said.

He shook his head. "Naw."

"You got an extra buck or two? I could use some help....for the baby. I need to see a doctor."

He pulled a ten from his pocket and put it on the counter. He thought it was a bad thing to give her money for crack, but not to give it to her would be just as bad. She would stand out on the street and beg for it or sell her body for it.

Al put Howie's burger on the counter. Howie ate, and then he went to look for Duke again. He walked back to all the old places, but he never found him.

About the Author

An award-winning fiction writer, Gay Rubin has had stories published in many literary journals, including *Iowa Woman*, *Iris*, *The Bridge* and *Metro Times*. The Arts Foundation of Michigan awarded her an individual artist's grant in 1994. She has been editor and founder of *Michigan Hot Apples* (an annual literary anthology of poetry and fiction), past president of Detroit Women Writers, and writing instructor at University of Michigan. She is currently host and producer of a new cable TV interview program, *Writers' Roundtable*, in Birmingham, Michigan, feature editor for *Cigar Lifestyles Magazine* and at work on a novel. Gay lives in Birmingham, Michigan, with her husband and two daughters.